THE AEROWYN TALES

Bellarose
AND THE
Pirate

CARLA REIGHARD

To book dragons looking for adventure and danger while staying at home.

To seekers of treasure and happiness:

For where your treasure is, there your heart will be also.

~ Luke 12:34

Acknowledgements

Thank you, Jenn & Marlee, for your suggestion on how Jasper should look. He's my first tattooed character.

Thank you, Cathy McCrumb, the best editor for this book!

Chapter 1

Jasper

The day Jasper led a mutiny, a gentle breeze blew the Black Fear's sails, but the sea only stirred where the ship sliced through it. Jasper's racing heart thumped in his chest, but his grip remained steady on his knife's hilt. His bare feet made almost no sound while he approached Captain Starr as the pock-faced man glared at a pod of dolphins on the starboard side.

"Don't take this personally," Jasper said as he deftly sliced the blade across the captain's throat.

The older man dropped to the deck, copper-scented crimson bubbling from his mouth.

Jasper's bloody weapon glinted in the sun. He stabbed it into the railing before he bent over the body.

"You taught me everything I needed to know to take this ship, but"—Jasper hoisted Starr with a grunt—"you forgot your most important lesson." He whispered in the dead man's ear, "*Never trust anyone.*"

His tattooed biceps flexed as he heaved the corpse over the side. Starr's body splashed into the water and bobbed for a while, but before the *Black Fear* had sailed far, the corpse sank beneath the billowing waves where it would be devoured by the ocean—or perhaps sirens.

After all, legends told of sirens who swam the oceans and wooed sailors into the water to feast on their hearts. Jasper paused. Were mermaids different from sirens? The fire-haired mergirl of his childhood dreams hadn't been vicious, only kind.

Bah! That's folklore and nonsense!

Jasper pulled a handkerchief from his pocket and wiped his hands clean. The late Captain Starr had been fond of saying, "No regrets and never look back."

That will be my next tattoo. I'll have it inked across my shoulder blades, so my enemies will see it as I leave them behind to rot.

"Is it finished, Cap'n?"

Jasper jerked around. The red-haired man looked from the bloody cloth to the water below, and Jasper drew a deep breath. Jeb's stealthy arrival had startled him, but he shoved any comparison of the sailor's sudden appearance to his attack on Starr aside. Now was not the time to allow anything to ruin his victory over putting Starr in Davy Jone's locker. Besides, Jeb was loyal. Jasper forced a smile.

"Yes, Jeb. Captain Starr has gone on a permanent leave to the bottom of the ocean."

"What next, Cap'n?"

Jeb's eager expression loosened the knots in Jasper's stomach. He pulled the knife free from the railing and straightened to his full height. He wouldn't let his guard down again, nor would he let the crew become dissatisfied with his leadership. He had learned from Starr's mistakes.

"Send Sven to me." Jeb left.

When footsteps slapped the deck behind him, Jasper pivoted, every sense alert.

The stout older man glanced around. "Jeb said the deed is finished."

"Yes."

"Aye Captain." Sven saluted. "Your orders, sir?"

"Sven, you are first mate now." Jasper wiped his knife and tucked his filthy handkerchief back in his pocket. "Assemble everyone."

"Aye aye, sir." Sven pivoted and blew a whistle.

Men of all sizes and shapes scuffled onto the upper deck. Murmurs rose. Sven quieted them, but when Jasper strode forward, his presence made the men fall silent.

"I am your new captain." Jasper made eye contact with each crew member. "Unlike Captain Starr, I won't flog, shackle, or keelhaul any without just cause. I will be fair. You will be given your rations and an equal share of the booty from raids, but—" Jasper raised his bass voice. "—if you disobey me or break any pirate code, there will be *no* second chances. Do I make myself clear?"

"Aye, Captain!" the men shouted in unison.

Some grinned in approval, and others gazed up at Jasper almost adoringly.

A voice rose from the back. "Ye've saved us from Starr!"

"And his insane punishments," someone else added.

Jasper ignored them and continued, "Everyone back to your duties! We sail until I choose our next course."

One of the men brought Jasper his belongings to the captain's quarters and he quickly discarded his blood-splattered clothes and replaced them with clean ones. He would adjust the space to his preferences later. First, he needed to let the day's events soak in, so he made his way to the quarterdeck to watch the sun sink into the waves. Up until now his restless spirit was never content, but now the wishes he had as a young lad on the *Black Fear* were finally coming to fruition.

I always said that someday I'd want for nothing and become too powerful to abuse. I'd never go hungry, never cower before anyone. Someday is finally here.

Jasper jumped slightly until he recognized the familiar, noisy steps that alerted him to the first mate's approach.

"What do you need, Sven?"

"I only wanted some fresh air."

Jasper tilted his head to eye the older man. "You have something on your mind."

Sven gulped. "I guess I do have some questions, but I didn't want to be disrespectful."

Jasper fought back a smirk. "Sven, did you know I was only seven when I first came aboard the *Black Fear?* Now look at me. At the age of twenty, I might be the youngest pirate captain on the sea."

"It is an amazing accomplishment, but..." The older man looked down and shuffled his feet.

"Spit it out. I promise you won't be punished."

Sven stood taller and looked straight into Jasper's eyes. "How did it feel to kill your mentor?"

Reminding himself that he'd promised no punishment for Sven's questions, Jasper clenched his fists.

His narrowed eyes glared at Sven. "What exactly do you expect to discover from your question?"

"Starr was the closest thing to a father you had. You were his favorite. Did you have to kill him?"

"You hadn't been around the former captain as long as I had been."

Sven swallowed hard. "True, but he spared me once I told him of Ageless Isle."

"Of course he did. You said it had untold wealth and the secret to immortality." Jasper shifted his weight. "He would have killed you with the rest of your crew if you hadn't bribed him. The fact that you're a healer, sealed the deal."

"I know, sir, but he was kind to me while I was on this ship."

"Captain Starr had become more unhinged than normal. He cut out Jack's left eye because he thought it had tried to cast an evil spell on him. Starr was always cruel like my own parents were." Jasper gripped the railing. "He beat me to teach me not to flinch, but that wasn't why I killed him."

"Then why?"

"Starr said he would kill every man in their sleep and get a new crew at the next port. He forgot our names, thought we were strangers. He was growing more dangerous because he feared the crew was out to murder him." Jasper's voice pitched low. "I hid his worst behavior from everyone, but I knew those closest to him saw the writing on the wall."

"Couldn't you have locked him in his room rather than kill him?"

Jasper huffed. "Pirates don't respect mercy. Our enemies wouldn't fear an interim captain. I had to usurp Starr in the same brutal way he had done with his predecessor to gain allegiance and reputation."

"So, you really were protecting us..." Sven rubbed a gold tear-shaped pendant that hung on a chain around his neck. "I understand." The stout man tucked the pendant back underneath his shirt and then smothered a yawn.

"If he went mad, we'd all be dead, myself included. Him or me? I'll always choose me." He rubbed his chin. "Get some rest, Sven."

"I will. Won't let you down, sir. Goodnight Captain."

Jasper glared up at the moon. Captain Starr had been right about one thing. Moral compass? No, the only compass a pirate needed was one that pointed north.

No regrets. Never look back.

Over the next year, the *Black Fear* carried out many successful raids. Jasper had replaced Starr's black flag bearing a skull with starred eye-sockets. Now, a white silhouette of a falcon on a black field boldly billowed on the mast. He smirked up at the symbol that had become synonymous with the cold-blooded Captain Falcon, the most successful pirate captain of the Caribbean.

Even so, discontent rose like storm clouds. Jasper glowered at the horizon. Sven's promise to lead them to Ageless Isle surfacing in his mind. Riches beyond measure and an immortal life. The Caribbean's wealth would be nothing in comparison. Maybe it was time to plan the trip.

Turning abruptly, Jasper made his way to his cabin, calling loudly for his first mate.

When the stocky man entered and shut the door, Jasper unrolled a map on his desk.

"Sven, how far is Ageless Isle from our current location?"

"Do you want me to summon the quartermaster to help chart a course, sir?"

"I don't want too many men aware of the destination until we're close to it."

"Very good, but it's a far sail." Sven bent over the map, then peered up at Jasper. "It would be wise to replenish our supplies first before heading to the island."

Jasper eyed the map. "We're close to the Port of New Orleans."

"Yes. We'll have to go to the Gulf and then channel through the Mississippi River here." Sven outlined the passage with his finger.

"Good. And it's the best place to trade and blend in. We can resupply and sell some of our valuable acquisitions." Jasper straightened. "All hands on deck."

"Aye, Captain."

Sven saluted and left, and Jasper headed to the quarterdeck to address the crew. Excitement drifted from the gathered men.

"What does Cap'n Falcon have planned now?"

"Must be somefin' real important to gather everyone."

"We already have more riches than I could have ever imagined!"

Jasper spoke above the din. "Men, it's time we start planning a new adventure."

Cheers erupted.

"We're heading toward Port of New Orleans to restock our supplies. We may be a little longer than usual to prepare for the journey ahead of us because we're going to an island none of us have seen before. Rumors say it holds great treasure." He raised his voice over the men's cheers. "Enjoy all the wenches you can while at port, because where we're going, you may not see one for a while."

Some men grunted, "Aye aye, Captain!"

A few chortled, and others made crude comments.

The illegally gained goods in the hold were offloaded and sold, and the quartermaster divided the profits. While the undisciplined men departed to squander their portions on ale and rum. Jasper stayed aboard. The ocean was his place of safety, and the ship was his home. He only planned to venture off the *Black Fear* to acquire food, liquor, and supplies for the voyage. After all, with the promise of ultimate wealth, he couldn't risk anyone else knowing their destination.

So, while Sven wrote in the log book coordinates to Ageless Isle and Jeb scrubbed the deck, Jasper pulled out his cutlass to practice lunges, but in the day's waning light, the hilt's cracked leather seemed worse.

Starr had promised that one day he would get Jasper a finely crafted saber with an ivory handle. He never had.

The words came out before he knew they were coming. "Do you know where I could get a new sword?"

Sven put down his log book. "Quinn, the blacksmith next to The Swan is said to be the best."

Jasper knew the easily intimidated proprietor of the place, and his lips curled in a half-smile. "Can this Quinn make a sword worthy of me?"

"He's an expert at crafting artistic but deadly blades."

"Yes, you know me well." Jasper sheathed the sword and patted the short, white-haired man on the back. "My weapon should produce fear and awe before my adversaries."

"It will, sir."

He grinned. "Maybe I can find a delicious lass for distraction after I commission the blade."

Jeb dropped the scrub brush into the bucket. "Cap'n, does that mean you'll be joinin' us at The Swan? It's full of the mos' beau'iful women in Orlins."

The most beautiful...

The words summoned the images he'd tried to suppress since childhood.

He shook his head. *Bah, if there was such a woman, maybe she could drive out the ghostly imaginations of fiery red hair and a glistening red tail.*

Something splashed into the water below and pulled Jasper out of his ponderings.

His voice full of admiration, Jeb prattled on. "They says a 'ero drinks there, but you could take 'im in a fight."

Jasper squinted at the copper-haired ship's tailor and gave an irritated half-shrug. "Of course, I could defeat some local hero. But business before pleasure. Sven, you have the ship. I'll commission a new sword first."

Sven waved a loose salute. "Best be going, sir. Craftmanship like Quinn's takes time."

Jasper might want a new sword, but Sven was right. He didn't want to delay the trip to the mysterious island any more than necessary. He strode down the gangplank and pushed through the crowds on the dock. A young boy pointed him in the direction of The Swan, and Jasper strode toward the stables.

The odors of straw, horse manure, hot metal and smoke made Jasper grimace. He much preferred the briny smells of the sea. Heat radiated from the blazing forge, several weapons of fine craftsmanship lodged in a rack nearby. This had to be the correct place.

But instead of a strapping blacksmith, the young man wearing the thick, leather apron was hunched unevenly, one shoulder blade jutting far above the other. He and an exquisite, green-eyed girl faced each other, swords in hand. She appeared to be only a few years younger than Jasper, who cringed at the sight of the beastly man next to the beauty.

"Blimey, you're hideous! Why didn't your mother suffocate you at birth?"

The green-eyed girl turned to face him. "You have dreadful manners!"

"My, my, what a lovely contrast you are to this thing." Jasper settled back on his heels and scanned her from head to toe. "You don't appear to be a prostitute. But why would a proper young lady want to be in its company?"

"You're despicable," she said through clenched teeth. "His name is Quinn, not 'it.'"

Quinn remained silent.

Jasper raised his eyebrows. "Anyway, deformed or not, I want Quinn to make me a magnificent sword." He faced the blacksmith. "Are you even able to?"

"Of course he can, but should he?" The beautiful girl stabbed her sword into a bale of straw.

"Is *he* attempting to teach you how to wield that weapon?" Jasper pointed to her sword. "My expert tutelage would be more fun. I *am* after all the captain of the *Black Fear*."

The spunky girl replied, "Should I be impressed?"

"I'm Captain Jasper Falcon. I know my reputation has reached New Orleans."

Her eyes widened in some kind of recognition, even though she shook her head and said, "I've never heard of you."

Jasper leaned toward Bella. Bar maids threw themselves at him, but well-bred young ladies cowered away. This girl's behavior was a pleasant change.

"Who are you?"

"It doesn't matter, because you will never get to know me." She scowled, and turned to bestow a smile on Quinn. "I will see you tomorrow for another lesson."

Quinn blushed. "I, um, I look forward to it."

The young man's smooth tenor took Jasper aback, as did the way the misshapen man focused on the girl as she disappeared from sight.

Jasper scowled. Anyone who looked like Quinn deserved to have something nasty to match his physique. Not love.

The disgusting man was obviously attracted to the girl. Who wouldn't be? She'd turn any man's head, if he weren't blind or stupid. Jasper was neither.

"Who is she?" he asked.

Quinn straightened. "None of your concern. You came to see me about a sword?"

Jasper's jaw ticced. No one refused to answer his questions, but if he were going to get that sword, he'd have to excuse the rudeness this one time. "You must lack practice with proper manners because you hide from people. If I looked like you, I wouldn't go out in public."

"I know who you are, Captain Falcon, but when it comes to Miss Bonnay, you need to stay away." Quinn hobbled inside the stable and returned the sword to a rack.

"Miss Bonnay, is it?" Jasper closed the distance between them. "Who is she to you that you are willing to risk your life for hers?"

"Are you threatening my life?" The smith's brown eyes narrowed, and his hand reached for the sword he'd just put up. "I may look disabled, but don't underestimate my abilities. I would gladly face you in a sword fight to defend Miss Bonnay's honor."

Jasper laughed. "The creature has confidence! I like it!" He rubbed his hands together. "Back to business. Yes, I want the finest sword you can make, and I'll pay you handsomely for it." He reached in his pocket and threw out a sack of gold coins at Quinn.

The bulging pouch jingled. Quinn barely caught it.

"If you want it to be a masterpiece, you will need to give me several weeks to craft it." Quinn pulled out two gold coins and threw the bag back at Jasper. "I'll take these for now and when you return for the sword, you can give me one more."

"Tell me where I can find Miss Bonnay, and I'll give you this entire purse." Jasper dangled the bag in the air. "If I don't like the sword, I won't ask you to return any of this."

Quinn held up the coins. "No, I'll only take these."

"It doesn't matter. I have ways of finding out what I want to know, and the beautiful Miss Bonnay's location will not elude me for long." Jasper turned to exit the stable. "Good day, ogre. I'll return in a few weeks for my sword."

Jasper sauntered away from the stench of the smithy and stable, well content with the transaction. Everything was working out.

He mentally ticked off the things he had accomplished since the mutiny. The crew was safe from the abuse of the long-dead Captain Starr. He'd gained admiration from many because of his fierce and fearless behavior. All that was left was permanent security and respect and that will be accomplished at Ageless Island, which promised riches beyond his imagination.

All was exactly how he had desired for himself. Jasper had everything he'd ever wanted.

Except for that mermaid.

His steps slowed. No. The dream had haunted his nightscapes too long, tempting him to care again, just when he couldn't afford sentimentality.

He was done with that. The mermaid wasn't real, but Miss Bonnay was.

It was time to replace the fictional girl with a real one.

Chapter 2

Bellarose

B ella's brows furrowed while she pulled herself onto the brown
mare's leather saddle. Maybe she shouldn't have left Quinn with
that wretched captain. She pulled back her shoulders and sighed. No,
he would be fine. He had defended her from more dangerous-looking
men when she had first arrived at Port New Orleans. He also shielded
her against a wolf. He could protect himself from that pirate. Though
he was eighteen like she was and had been alone most of his life, he was
an excellent swordsman. She hid a smile at the thought, even though no
one was looking. His swordsmanship was another reason he impressed
her. There wasn't a good reason to be vexed about his safety.

The damp wind cut through her black cloak, and she shivered, even
though the temperatures in Louisiana never dropped as low as they
did in France, where—

*Visions of a snow-dusted oval of ice, strange flashing lights, and loud
music danced across her memory.*

Bella blinked rapidly. What was that besides unfamiliar and
strange?

She shrugged off the images. Her vivid dreams and fanciful storybooks must have leaked into her reality again, but at least they distracted her fretting over Quinn and that pirate.

What was it about black-haired, blue-eyed men that made them arrogant jerks? Captain Falcon and Gerard were exceptionally attractive

men, but both had behaved atrociously. Their arrogant swarthiness was a contrast to Quinn's sweet demeanor and his auburn hair and warm brown eyes.

Bella urged the horse into the sharp wind.

To be fair, Gerard's willingness to become a wolf to break Aerowyn's curse on his brother redeemed him from his previous flaws. That transformation changed her opinion of the man. Captain Falcon's sinister smugness, however, scared her.

Bella dropped off the horse at the Rose Manor stable, and a servant led the animal away. Bella's thoughts of Quinn, Gerard, and the nasty pirate, however, were interrupted when her friend Brooke called her name.

"Bella! Where have you been?"

"I went to see Quinn. He's teaching me swordplay."

Brooke's frown melted away, and her eyes sparkled. "I still can't imagine why a girl would need to learn about such things, but I suppose it gives you an excuse to see Quinn."

Bella's face warmed. "Possibly."

"Not to change the subject, but I need your expertise." Grabbing the corner of Bella's cloak, Brooke tugged her to the house. "I need you to help me choose a dress for the wedding."

She pulled Bella past the kitchen with all its tantalizing aromas. Her haste only made Bella smile. Antoine had asked Brooke to marry him on the same day the year-long curse was broken, and Brooke was in a frenzy over wedding plans.

"Here." Brooke led Bella to her room with a wardrobe full of dresses Antoine's mother had never worn. The young bride's cheeks blushed. "I pulled out several gowns I thought would be appropriate, but I can't decide."

"And you want Antoine to be overwhelmed when he sees you," Bella teased.

Her friend's cheeks grew even rosier. "Well, it is our wedding."

Bella eyed the gowns Brooke had placed onto the bed, then turned back to the wardrobe and grabbed a different. Dress. Cream-colored rose-shaped buttons and intricate lace adorned the silk gown's tightly fitted bodice. The long elegant sleeves' cuffs frothed with lace, and the skirt flowed to the floor in graceful folds.

"This one," Bella said. "*This* is the perfect dress."

Brooke brushed her hand over the material. "Ohh... Yes, it is."

Bella beamed, but then her smile faltered. Since Gerard sacrifice had made this happen, Bella wished he could witness the ceremony as a man. Brooke and Antoine had found their happy ending, just like as characters in one of Bella's books, but—

An oversized book's flapping pages flashed in Bella's memory.

She grabbed the side of the wardrobe for balance.

The happy awe on Brooke's face vanished, and her forehead furrowed. "What's wrong?"

"Nothing," Bella said hurriedly. "I was only recalling a strange dream. Sometimes they hit me whenever I think of fairy tale endings like the one you and Antoine are finally going to have."

"It is like a dream." Brooke sighed, her concern fading away. "Perhaps, you'll have one with Quinn someday."

Bella's stomach flip-flopped. "I don't know anything about that." Her friend's words brought the awful interruption to her visit with Quinn to mind, and she frowned. "Have you heard of Captain Jasper Falcon?"

Brooke shook her head. "No. Who is he?"

"I guess you wouldn't have heard of his reputation since you were under a curse. When I worked at The Swan, some of the patrons mentioned how thankful they were that Gerard's presence scared off pirates. That captain's name came up more than once."

"Pirates," Brooke gasped. "In our town?"

"Yes." Bella took off her cloak and set it aside before hanging the other dresses in the wardrobe. "Their fights demolished so many establishments, and most of The Swan's regulars are decent folk looking for reprieve. No one dares get in the way of such murderers, so they tend to get whatever they want."

Brooke gasped. "That doesn't sound like a safe place."

"Quinn was always nearby to rescue me." Bella sighed. "Anyway, Gustave—Quinn's father—didn't appreciate their patronage because he lost money and customers whenever they visited. It's one of the many reasons he was glad for Gerard's presence. He kept the pirates at bay. Not even a cutthroat wanted to cross a war hero. So, despite his arrogance, he attracted the right customers. I guess that's why when I slapped him, I lost my job."

Brooke gaped at her. "You *slapped* him?"

"Yes," she said hastily, "but in my defense, he had pulled me onto his lap."

"Well, that was bad form." Brooke dismissed Gerard's behavior and scooped up the wedding dress. "But he sacrificed his humanity to save all of us, and I will never think poorly of him again. Besides, he rescued you from pirates in a round-about way."

"I know."

Both fell silent for a few minutes.

Bella closed the wardrobe door and leaned against it. A shiver ran through her.

"Today, the infamous Captain Falcon returned and asked Quinn to make him a sword. I was late and had to leave, so I didn't stay to hear them discuss it. The captain looked at me like I was his next meal after days without food. It was unnerving." Her jaw clenched. "He also called Quinn names."

"That's horrible," Brooke said. "Perhaps while the pirates are in town you should stay clear of that pub."

"But I want to see Quinn again."

Brooke hummed thoughtfully. "Maybe Antoine can spare one of the servants to accompany you next time. And you must invite him to the wedding as your special guest." Brooke raised one eyebrow. "Tell him we forgive him for almost killing my betrothed."

Bella covered her face. "I should have told him about the enchantment on the plantation. Although, none of us knew Antoine would turn into a wolf in front of the guests."

"I think Aerowyn did that on purpose to force a decision to break the curse." Brooke headed to the door. "I want to hang this up in my room before Antoine sees it."

Bella followed, but her thoughts remained on Brooke's words. "Aerowyn is a powerful enchantress, not a future teller. Could she have traveled into the future to see how the story played out?" Bella stopped that line of thought. It could lead back to her strange dreams. "Anyway, the curse is broken, and you and Antoine will marry soon. I feel like an interloper. You don't really need me after the wedding."

"You're not an interloper," Brooke protested. "I know nothing on how to be an aristocrat's wife. You're helping me with that and the wedding." She hung up the dress and motioned Bella to sit next to her on the bed.

"I'm not an aristocrat anymore. I need to earn my keep."

Brooke wrapped an arm around Bella. "My life has changed as well. I'm not sure what will happen once Antoine and I are married." Her eyes took on a far-off look. "I wasn't supposed to marry rich. My future only held hard work."

Bella laughed lightly. "And I was supposed to marry rich and rely on my husband to take care of everything."

"Life has a way of turning upside-down."

"It does." Bella stood. "But change is inevitable no matter who you are, and speaking of change, I need to get ready for dinner."

She gave her friend a quick hug and darted out before Brooke could say anything else. Allowing her longing for a happy ending like Antoine and Brooke would only lead to discontent, but until she figured out what to do next, she'd continue to help Brooke with hers.

As she passed the library doors, a vision of a similar place made her breath hitch. Escaping into fairy tales had always comforted her, but this time the room filled with tomes put her on edge.

As long as vile men like Captain Falcon interfered in their lives, a blissful conclusion to whatever story awaited her and Quinn seemed like a fairy tale.

Chapter 3

Jasper

True to his word, Jasper stormed into The Swan on a mission to learn more about the beautiful Miss Bonnay. Round, wooden tables and short-backed chairs filled the center of the tavern, and several patrons devoured turkey legs and bread. Jasper's stomach growled, but he ignored it.

Wooden benches and longer tables sat in the corners. Men called for bar maids, who sloshed mugs of cider into the tables. The raucous jeers and singing stopped one by one, the people observed Jasper's presence. He puffed his chest and headed to the bar where a tall man with graying brown hair slowly wiped a tankard with a square cloth. The proprietor of The Swan hadn't changed much.

"Captain Falcon! It's been a while since I've seen you in these parts." His eyes darted between Jasper and the other patrons. "How can I help you?"

Jasper approached the proprietor. "Gustave, my fine fellow. I'll have whatever that man is drinking." He threw a coin onto the counter and pointed to the short older man who hung over the bar.

Gustave filled a mug and put it in front of Jasper.

He swigged the drink and then said, "I was just commissioning a sword from your son and met a fine lass, but neither she nor your son would tell me her name."

The man's thick neck turned red. "Captain, please accept my most humble apology. How can I make it up to you? For obvious reasons, my son doesn't—"

Jasper bared his teeth and narrowed his eyes. "I assume he lacks manners because of his infirmity, but if you can tell me anything about this Miss Bonnay, then all will be forgiven."

"Miss Bonnay?" Gustave turned his head toward the entrance. "Was she outside?"

"Yes. Your son was teaching her swordsmanship."

The older man pounded his fist on the bar. "That girl is trouble. Her name is Bellarose Bonnay, but she likes to be called Bella. She's from France, where her now deceased father gambled away all their riches. I gave her a job to be charitable, but she acted too high and mighty for my customers. She was a horrible bar wench, but the last straw was when she insulted Gerard." Gustave pursed his lips. "He was one of my best patrons and a war hero, which is why I told her she no longer worked for me. If I'd known Quinn had befriended her, I would have put a stop to it immediately."

Jasper smirked. So, the girl had been rude to the so-called debonair war hero, Gerard. If she didn't like handsome or powerful men, maybe Jasper could persuade her with something else. He liked a challenge, because even looting and killing could become predictable. Conquering her would be extremely satisfying. He only had to figure out what motivated her.

"Gustave, where do you think Bella went? I may be able to hire her to *work* on my ship."

The bar owner flinched. "I-I know you're a persuasive man, but don't be surprised if she rejects your offer." Gustave wiped his brow. "I heard rumors she is currently a servant at the de la Rose plantation,

Rose Manor. The Count and Countess died and left the place to their son."

Jasper scooted the mug over the bar and then pulled on the cuffs of his shirt. That son had better not mind losing a servant because Jasper's restless interest was piqued. For a split second, a fantastical mermaid with a call to the sea bobbed into his mind's eye. *Bah!* He rubbed his eyes to erase the vision. Bella was flesh and bone. She would replace the illusion.

"How can I get acquainted with the new master of the plantation?"

Gustave filled a mug with ale as he replied. "Rumors said the plantation is haunted and that the young Antoine is a recluse. He never comes into town, nor does he have visitors. How Bella managed to get inside the doors is beyond me."

As if that would frighten Jasper. Ghosts weren't real, and plenty of reclusive, wealthy men had already died by his sword. "I'd like to visit this place to see if the story is true."

Gustave stopped pouring ale. "In fact, that's where Gerard has been. He's the heir's twin, though that was only recently discovered. I haven't seen Gerard since the fancy ball they held, but I've heard of some strange happenings there."

Jasper snorted, then leaned back and eyed Gustave. The burly owner of The Swan sounded like an old, gossiping bitty, but could Gerard be a competitor for Bella's affections? She insults him and then becomes his servant—curious. Although, Gerard may be punishing her for her insolence.

Finally, he asked, "Where is this plantation located?"

"Outside of town." Gustave handed the full mug to a maid, then grabbed an empty one and started pouring again. "You can't miss it, but if you do, anyone from around these parts should be able to point you in the right direction."

Restocking the *Black Fear* would take a few weeks, and having Quinn finish his sword would take about that long. Still, Jasper preferred to steal opportunities rather than leave things to chance. He may run into Bella Bonnay again in town, but patience wasn't his virtue. He needed to craft an opportunity she couldn't reject and to set the plan into motion.

Yes, the more he thought about it, the more he knew Bella would be the perfect satisfying distraction aboard the *Black Fear*. She would fill lonely nights between plundering ships, and when they docked at islands, he'd only need to leave the ship to barter for supplies. If his first mate handled the resupply, he wouldn't have to set foot on shore again.

I need to make an offer she can't refuse, but if she does, kidnapping is the best option.

An idea began to take shape, and he tossed another coin on the counter. "Another ale, Gustave."

The bar keep slid a mug to him, and he threw back half the drink in one swallow.

A voluptuous bar maid leaned close and said breathlessly, "Can I get the fine captain another drink?"

"Aye." Jasper smiled and slapped her bum as she turned.

The girl giggle, but then Bella's scowl popped into his head. Something about that young woman got under his skin.

Mutiny is one thing, but this idea? Genius.

He folded his arms across his chest.

Pure genius. I'll never have to step foot on land again.

After ten days of being at port, Jasper paced the quarterdeck while Sven charted the course to Ageless Isle. There was an ornate captain's chair near the wheel, but he didn't feel like sitting. Sven was huddled over the navigation table mapping out the way.

The older man put down his sextant. "Why do you hate the land?"

Jasper stopped mid-stride. "I never said that I hate it."

"No, but you stay on the ship even when it's docked. You only leave to tend to necessary business."

"You stay on the ship almost as much as I do." Jasper crossed his arms. "Does that mean you detest land?"

Sven shook his head. "I'm too old to carouse like the others. I might as well stay aboard ship like a little old lady. What's your excuse?"

"You're right. I'm ready to leave New Orleans behind." When Sven waited patiently, Jasper bit off a sigh. "Ports remind me of my childhood. This ship was my escape, though Captain Starr didn't treat me much better than my own folks had. The sea became a refuge." Jasper sat down. "Everyone on the *Black Fear* knew if they worked hard enough and obeyed Starr's orders, they could forget their pasts."

"That makes sense why you stay on the ship." Sven cleared his throat. "Then you'll be happy to know we almost have all the supplies we need for the long journey. We could leave as soon as you give the orders."

"You're right. But, I'm waiting on two things." Jasper stood and put on his jacket. "First, I need to check with Quinn about my sword."

Jasper left the *Black Fear* without telling Sven what that second thing was, but he tramped the sodden streets to the smithy to check on Quinn's progress, his thoughts strayed to Bella. Not only would the island's rare treasures be worth the quest, but whispers also said that the island really granted immortality. If he had both riches and lived forever, maybe he could share his life with a woman like Bella. Jasper pushed aside the question of where that idea came from and stepped a little quicker.

Loud clanks sounded through the wide-open smithy doors. There, Quinn was pounding hot metal over the anvil. The horseshoe sizzled when he dipped it into a barrel of water. Jasper strode in. A quick glance at the workmanship of the blades on the walls showed the deformed man's reputation was justified. He was a true artist in his craft.

"I will say for a man of your challenges, your work surprises me. How is the progress going with my sword?"

Tight-lipped, Quinn eyed him, crossed to a table, and picked up a blade by the tang. He handed it to Jasper who placed the mostly finished sword horizontal across his palms to get a feel of its weight and balance, even without the hilt. The metal shone brightly against the sun, and the blade looked sharp enough to slice a hair. The finished sword would truly invoke fear and admiration from his foes.

He nodded in satisfaction. "When will you complete it?"

"The only step left is, um, to attach the hilt to the blade. I could finish it today or tomorrow if I'm not interrupted." Quinn picked up the sword's separate handle. "I like to make the hilt look like a piece of art but have it comfortable to hold."

Jasper clicked his tongue. "You know, I think your talents are being wasted here. Your father hides you away in these stalls instead of giving you the chance to show off your true abilities."

Quinn glanced skeptically at Jasper. "What exactly do you think my true abilities are? It seems all you see is my deformity."

"I see more than that." It wasn't a complete lie. "You have all the components required for a fine sailor. I could easily make you rich aboard my ship, and you wouldn't need to grovel or hide like you do here." Jasper set the unfinished blade down and let the idea hang in the air.

After all, there was a chance Bella would willingly join his crew if Quinn was aboard. Jasper could dispose of the monster easily enough. If she refused, this offer would provide plan an alibi.

"There was a time when I thought I wanted to get as far away from this place as I could. I even considered sailing," the hunchbacked man said, "but now I find New Orleans isn't such a terrible place after all."

Jasper chortled. "Even though you have told me nothing about the lovely Bellarose, could she be the reason you want to stay?"

Quinn scowled. "Who told you her name?"

"Your father. He said where I could find her. He also explained that she has no family and is a pauper." Jasper smiled widely. "I think I could benefit you both."

"She doesn't need help from the likes of you," Quinn said through gritted teeth.

"But she needs you?" Jasper eyed the lad who looked a few years younger than he was. "What could you possibly offer a girl who came from wealth and grandeur? Now she's living at one of the most prosperous plantations of the south. Eventually, she will meet a wealthy suitor and get married. She will no longer need a pathetic bowed man to fight her battles for her."

Quinn's fingers tightened around the grip. "She's not that kind of girl."

"You mean the kind who likes to be lavished in jewels and silks and knows she will never want for anything?" Jasper flashed a crooked grin. "Tell me you can keep her satisfied, because I have yet to meet a girl from an aristocratic background who wouldn't think twice about accepting a marriage proposal from a man who could spoil her with the luxuries she's been surrounded by all her life."

The misshapen young man eyed him suspiciously. "What are you getting at?"

"I'm only saying if you think she won't eventually tire of you, then you are more delusional than deformed. On the other hand, you could join my crew and become rich beyond belief. You would return to New Orleans in a year or two and give Bellarose all the riches she deserves. At that point, maybe she'd be ecstatic to marry you."

"I don't want to leave her behind." The blacksmith gave him a venomous gaze. "She needs my protection from scoundrels like you."

"What if I told you I visited her at the plantation?" Jasper turned his attention back to the incomplete sword but kept watch on Quinn out of the corner of his eye. "I offered her the life she is suited for, and she agreed to join me as my guest in the captain's suite aboard my ship."

"What?"

Jasper turned back to the enraged blacksmith and flashed a toothy grin. "I promised her that after I find the mysterious Ageless Isle with all its riches, we'll settle as husband and wife in a mansion on a palatial estate. After all, she isn't the kind of girl who wants to sail the seas forever."

"You're lying!" Quinn said tautly. "She wouldn't travel with a band of pirates to marry an affluent man."

"Woah, settle down." Jasper raised his hands in surrender. "I'm not going to sully her. I will sleep in a different cabin. She correctly believes I'm a gentleman privateer, not a nasty pirate, no matter what others say." Jasper dipped his head in false humility. "I can't help it that she also thinks I'm handsome. Whether she loves me or not, my attractiveness will prevent our union from being totally repulsive to her."

"I'm sure many women think you're alluring, but she isn't concerned about riches any longer. It will take more than a striking man to sway her, and besides, she told me that she likes a simple life now."

"She didn't have a choice when she was a bar maid for your father. She had to learn how to be content when there were no other options." When the other man slumped, Jasper suppressed a grin. That wasn't a true lie, or at least from the other man's sagging shoulders, Jasper's words struck a sore spot. Renewed confidence prompted him to continue, "I'm sure once she started helping out at the de la Rose plantation, she got a renewed taste for a more decadent way of living. Now Bella wants to go back to the extravagances she once had, and I can give them to her.

"I'm a fair man. I'll give you a chance to win her heart. Become part of my crew and gain your own prosperity. If she decides she loves you instead of me, I'll give her up willingly. No interference."

Lips pursed, Quinn listened, and the wheels were obviously turning in his head.

As if in afterthought, Jasper added, "If she ends up loving me instead, I will let you leave the ship with your fortune. If Bella can't decide which one she prefers after you've become wealthy, then we can duel for her."

Quinn cleared his throat. "I should, um, talk to Bella before I decide."

Apprehension sneaked past Jasper's confidence. His plan wouldn't work if Quinn talked to Bella before he did.

"Is that because you don't totally trust me?"

"Partially. Your reputation isn't the best around this town, but then—" the smith studied Jasper, then shrugged"—I'm not judged fairly by anyone who sees me either. Rumors could be incorrect about you, too, and if you are as persuasive as you seem, I supposed it's possible that Bella changed her mind."

"Ultimately, it wasn't me. It was the promise of a better life that convinced her." Jasper made a show of obviously eyeing the other man up and down. "In your own way—if only one could ignore your defects—you're somewhat handsome. But you need to be able to offer Bella all she deserves."

Quinn readjusted his stance. "Even if what you're saying to me is true, it doesn't make sense. Why would you want to give me a chance to win Bella's heart and risk losing her?"

"Maybe we aren't soul-mates." Jasper managed to keep from gagging at the notion. "Time aboard my ship will give us all a chance to see who is suited to whom."

"I still want to talk to her first. She's always been honest with me. I trust her more than I'll ever trust you."

"Suit yourself, but this is a one-time offer. I'm being very generous to allow you to come aboard my ship with your obvious flaws." Jasper motioned to Quinn's back. "Can you even do the same work a normal man can?"

Quinn huffed. "I keep up just fine. A humped back doesn't stop me from doing anything. It only keeps people from seeing me as a man."

"I'll give you until midnight to let me know what you decide, and then I rescind the offer. That's when I want my sword ready." Jasper pivoted to exit the stables but glimpsed at Quinn over his shoulder. "Once the ship leaves with Bellarose, you'll lose all opportunities to win her affections."

He left Quinn to contemplate his lies. All Jasper needed was for both of them to trust his words without speaking to each other. Once Bella was on his ship, no one would chase after her. If Quinn joined them, he'd dispose of the creature while they were in the middle of the ocean.

Jasper sauntered out of the hot stables and breathed in the cleaner manure-free air. In New Orleans's crowded streets, no one paid attention to him. After he walked a few blocks, he came upon a tavern with a horse was tied out front. Convenient and lucky. Jasper *borrow*ed it to visit the de la Rose plantation.

The trip offered no obstacles, and Gustave had been right. It was easy to find. When Jasper arrived, the house was bustling with activity. Maids and butlers cheerfully tied satin white bows around the oak trees that lined the long driveway to the mansion.

A trim brunette dressed in plain clothes was decorating the front doors with fragrant multi-colored roses when he rode up and slid off the horse.

"Good day," he began.

She turned to face him.

"I'm Captain Jasper Falcon of the—" He stopped himself. The *Black Fear* sounded too much like a pirate ship. "*The Opportune.* I've come to speak to Miss Bonnay, if she's available."

"Captain Falcon?" The lovely young woman squinted. "I'm Brooke. From what I've heard, you're a pirate. I doubt Miss Bonnay would like to speak to you."

He bowed. "Madame, I assure you the rumors about me are false. I'm a privateer of the strictest morals who makes a living trading and selling goods that I transport from faraway lands."

She looked him up and down. "I suppose she'll be safe. Bella is in the rose garden setting up chairs for our wedding. She's surrounded by people including my betrothed. You can't harm her."

Jasper dipped his head. "I only have honorable intentions for Miss Bonnay. I wish I could meet the scoundrel who sullied my reputation. I would fight him in a duel."

She frowned. "Follow the pathway that leads around back."

As he navigated his way to the back yard, he chuckled at his obvious lie. He recognized Bella at once, despite the work dress much like the ones the house staff wore. She still looked exquisite. For a moment, the possibility of retiring from pirating after he visited Ageless Isle darted through Jasper's mind.

If he were wealthy, he could afford a place like this one, and possibly settle down with a wife and child.

His muscles tensed, and he shook his head. *Bah!* Those were ridiculous, unrealistic notions. His childhood was proof of that. The sea was the only place he felt joy. It was home.

Bella wouldn't be his downfall. She was merely a diversion.

Servants milled around setting up chairs and digging a pit to roast a pig. In the distance, a tall, muscular blond-haired man watched him closely but didn't approach. Given his fine clothing, he was probably the master of the estate.

Focus on your goals, Jasper.

He forced what he hoped was an easy smile onto his face and approached Bella. "Miss Bonnay."

Bella glowered at him. "What are you doing here?"

"The future lady of the house directed me this way when I told her reports about me being a pirate were false and that I wanted to talk to you." He turned his head to the mansion. "She mentioned you weren't alone, but I have no wish to harm you."

Bella returned to her work. "I have no desire to talk to you. Leave now!"

He walked in front of her to force her to make eye contact. "Please hear me out before you dismiss me." When she moved away, Jasper held up his hands. "I promise I will make it worth your time. It's about Quinn."

Bella looked up sharply. "Did you hurt Quinn?"

"Of course not."

Her brows furrowed, and then she motioned him away from the other servants. Even in her perturbed state, she was lovely.

She put her hands on her hips. "I'll give you five minutes."

"Well then, I'd better be concise." Jasper winked, and she rolled her eyes. Then he spoke rapidly, as if he feared he wouldn't be able to get through the words. "I want to make Quinn a sailor aboard my ship. I felt badly for how I treated him, and well..." Jasper pinched his lips, then lowered his voice. "Even though he is a man, his father beats him."

Bella nodded, and her face paled.

"When I was a child, my parents beat me, so I ran away to become a sailor at a young age." His words ground to a halt, and his heart raced.

He'd meant to tell her that much because mixing truths with falsehoods made the lies more convincing, but at that second, the hidden truth cut deep. Parents should protect their children. The wound—stung afresh, even after all these years. A sudden urge struck him as hard as a blow—*confess to someone—to Bella—that was the real reason I murdered Captain Starr. The Black Fear's men are my family, and I was tired of standing by while an unstable tyrant abused them.*

Bellas' expression softened.

With a grunt, Jasper shook off his pain. He clenched his jaw, then forced it to relax. "To help Quinn out, I offered him a way to escape his father, but he refused me because he loves you. He told me he won't leave you behind." He winced—anther part of his lie, although a pretty obvious truth as far as that pathetic smith was concerned. Her cheeks flushed prettily, and Jasper' confidence returned.

He added softly, "Don't tell him I told you. I'm sure he wants to articulate that in his own way."

"Oh," she breathed.

Jasper fought back a smile.

"I asked about you after seeing you with Quinn. I heard about your parents. I'm sorry for your loss." He paused while Bella wiped one eye. "I thought I could help you too. I know a ship full of rough men isn't what a lady like yourself is accustomed to, but if you board my ship as a guest in the captain's suite, Quinn would join my crew."

Her whole demeanor changed, and she narrowed her eyes. "Where would you sleep if I'm in your room?"

"I'd kick the first mate out of his quarters. He can bunk with the rest of the crew."

She looked skeptical.

"What's in this for you?"

The next lie had to be his most convincing yet.

"I'm desperate to have a good man like Quinn aboard my ship. I lost some crew members to New Orleans when they decided to settle here, and my weapons expert died. Since Quinn is an excellent swordsman, he would be a perfect addition."

Her head tilted slightly. One brow arched. "That sounds almost too convenient. I trusted my own father, and he betrayed me. I don't trust easily." Bella bit her lip. "Also, you mocked Quinn like he was some kind of animal, and now you believe he'll be a valuable member of your crew?"

Jasper frowned. "When I made fun of him, I was in a foul mood after losing more crew members. That's not a good excuse, but I'm a flawed man." He put his palms together and pleaded, "Please forgive my bad behavior. We need Quinn. Privateers must be able to defend their ship against pirates."

"And you think that I will be safe?"

Jasper slightly nodded. *As safe as anyone can be on a ship full of pirates.*

"I'm not trying to scare you," he said. "If Quinn helped me get to my next destination unharmed, he would become rich along with all my crew. Then you two could settle down somewhere and live happily ever after."

The fairy tale phrase nearly turned his stomach, so he added, "Truthfully, I think it would be better to leave you here to wait for our return, but even after the promise of riches beyond imagination, Quinn refuses to leave you behind."

Bella's blush confirmed Jasper's assumptions.

"When Quinn refused, I thought that maybe you could help around our ship. Perhaps give it a woman's touch. I promise not one of my men will lay a hand on you. Quinn will enforce that promise as well."

The lies rolled easily off his tongue, even though Bella still glowered at him, she didn't demand that he leave. She was considering his proposal.

And that meant victory would be his.

Chapter 4

Bellarose

Bella didn't trust Captain Jasper Falcon, no matter what he said. She watched him so intently that the backdrop of the forest, the manicured boxwood hedges, and the serenity of the geometric pathways and dormant plants, disappeared with the captain's presence.

He said he wasn't a pirate, but over a week ago, he had criticized Quinn for his appearance, which seemed more pirate than privateer behavior. It wasn't proof, but was also true local tales and gossip weren't always factual. Stories about Gerard had definitely been exaggerated, even though everyone had believed them to be accurate. After Gerard and Bella had made amends, he admitted that Leo, his friend and fellow soldier, had stretched the truth about his battlefield heroics. Perhaps the tales of Captain Falcon were incorrect, too, but even so, he had bad manners.

Still, he had apologized for his awful words...

Her thoughts in turmoil, she returned to setting up the chairs for the wedding while she considered the captain's words. To her surprise, he joined her in the task.

But, did that make him trustworthy?

She sighed. She had been looking for a way to leave the de la Rose plantation after the wedding. Captain Falcon's offer sounded too good to be legitimate, but the idea that Quinn loved her and wouldn't leave her behind made her heart race. Her insides warmed, and her mood soared.

She'd never said the word love a loud when talking about Quinn. Yet, she didn't want a life without him in it. That was probably love, but she was afraid of admitting it until she heard him say he loved her.

And if she left on that ship, not only would she be giving herself a new life, but she would be helping Quinn escape his horrible father. She didn't want to be the reason Quinn stayed in New Orleans. This was the perfect solution for both of them—and that made her extremely skeptical.

She spun to face the captain and asked, "When are you leaving New Orleans?"

"As soon as Quinn finishes my sword." He stopped moving chairs. "I only stayed this long because I need a new blade. I won't be returning here in the near future. Maybe never. It depends on if the reports of Ageless Isle are true."

She was about to grab a chair and stopped. "Is that the name of the place you are going?"

"Yes, supposedly the people of the island have their own word for it, but no one else can pronounce it."

While the captain moved the last chair into the row, Bella stood off to the side to see if anything else needed to be done. Everything was in place.

She faced the man and folded her arms. "What reports have you heard about this Ageless Isle?"

"It is said to be loaded with a treasure of spices, jewels, and other rare objects. Some may even say it has magic."

Magic. Bella's pulse quickened. Before her journey over the Atlantic Ocean, she would've scoffed at any reference to the supernatural, but now she knew it existed. She had seen it firsthand with the enchantress's spell on Antoine's household before Gerard had broken the curse, but again, it sounded too good to be true.

"It sounds intriguing, especially for someone like me who loves to read books about such locations." His swarthy smile grew bigger, but she ignored it. "I want to talk to Quinn first before I agree to join you."

Jasper's smile disappeared. "You're not going to tell him I let his secret out about loving you, are you?"

"No, of course not!" Bella's cheeks warmed. "I'm not entirely sure you're trustworthy on that topic, but I want him to confirm that you actually offered him a job. You are correct that I may need to find a new situation for my own life after Antoine and Brooke marry, but they aren't rushing me out."

"Make sure you decide before midnight. I told Quinn to have my sword finished by then and that my offer for him to join my crew would expire then. We sail tonight."

Something sounded wrong with the way he seemed to be pushing her for a decision without allowing her time to think, but she wasn't accustomed to privateers and their ways. Maybe that was how ships worked. When she and her parents had crossed the Atlantic Ocean, sailors had spoken of tides in a most confusing manner. Since Quinn was invited also, it was imperative that she talk to him before deciding. The wedding was tomorrow, but Brooke and Antoine would have a wonderful ceremony with or without her presence.

"Fine. I'll let you know before midnight," she assured the captain. "In the meantime, I have a wedding to prepare for, and I still need to go into town to talk to Quinn."

Jasper bowed. "Then I bid you adieu and appreciate your consideration."

He strode off, leaving Bella to her racing thoughts. The promise of adventure brought joy bubbling to the surface.

Maybe her dead-end prospects were improving after all.

Chapter 5

Jasper

J asper rode back to town and returned the animal where he had found it. He had zero conscience about stealing it in the first place, but there was no reason to keep the beast, not where he was going.

He'd give Quinn a final chance to join him on the journey, but if the man refused, Bella couldn't know that. He did, however, need a way to snatch Bella before she talked to Quinn. His false knowledge of the trip was to provide an alibi, to avoid Bella's wealthy friends from coming after her. Jasper commandeered a carriage and re-visited Quinn.

Inside the stable, the monster polished Jasper's blade as a finishing touch.

"Smithy, I see you completed my sword. Well done."

"Yes, but I haven't been able to talk to Bella yet." Quinn made short strides toward Jasper and handed him the weapon. "I will not be able to give you an answer until we talk." He cleared his throat. "But, um, currently, I'm inclined to stay in New Orleans."

Fool. Jasper schooled his expression to keep the sneer from emerging. "If you don't show up at the dock by midnight, I'll take that as your rejection to my proposal." He handed Quinn two more gold coins. "Per our agreement for payment. Goodnight, unless we meet again."

Instead of heading back to the *Black Fear*, Jasper waited near the public house. As the sun dipped below the horizon, the streets emptied. Everyone went home or was enjoying refreshments in the pubs. His crew gathered in The Swan, which became raucous as they enjoyed their last night in New Orleans. Jasper's confidence rose. The noise provided cover. He kept his attention on the streets and waited.

As expected, Bella arrived. Her horse trotted up to The Swan, and she dismounted. While she was hitching the beast to a post, Jasper grabbed her and clamped his hand over her mouth. She writhed in his strong grasp. The perfume of roses and fear mixed in the air.

Intoxicating.

"If you scream," he hissed in her ear, "Quinn will die."

Bella's body turned rigid against his.

"Don't struggle." He said hoarsely. "You can't overpower me. You will only get yourself hurt. If you join my crew, I guarantee Quinn will follow. If you refuse to cooperate, I'll kill Quinn before he knows we're even here."

Her red face and wild look reminded Jasper of a trapped animal. For a split second, memories of his parents restraining him tried to stop him, but her very faint nod erased that temptation. Instead, a rush of superiority gave him added resolve.

He dragged her away from her horse before tying a scarf around her mouth. After tossing her into the back of the carriage, he bound her arms and legs. Escape would be impossible. He hopped to the seat and snapped the reins. The carthorse jerked into action.

Music from one of the more crowded bars filled the air, along with the mouth-watering aroma of smoked meat turning over a kitchen fire. Jasper's stomach grumbled, and he grabbed a small flask from his coat pocket and took a swig of rum to quiet it.

The journey to Jasper's ship wasn't long, and fortunately, they didn't pass anyone.

Only a few sailors loitered around the docks, but their presence didn't bother him when he pulled the horse to a stop. Leaving the reins dangling, he jumped down, wrenched open the door, and released Bella.

"If you scream," he growled, "I'll squeeze your throat until you faint."

Her eyes widened, and she nodded. He removed the gag. She didn't make a peep. Then he hoisted her over his shoulder and smacked her on her backside.

"She had a little too much to drink," he said when one of the sailors seemed interested.

They chuckled, made vulgar comments, and returned to their own tasks.

She mumbled, but he squeezed her threateningly. He whisked Bella to his quarters without arousing any alarm, gagged her again, and secured her to the bed. She struggled against the bonds. The lamp light shone upon her tear-stained face and mussed hair. She appeared bedraggled and forlorn.

"My dear Bellarose, please stop moving about like a fish out of water. You'll get rope burns on that delicate, fair skin." Jasper lightly brushed a finger over her wrist. "I need you to do me a huge favor, but it will actually help Quinn out the most. If you refuse me, I will kill Quinn as I promised earlier."

Her teary eyes widened.

Jasper clicked his tongue. "There's no need to cry. If you cooperate with me, Quinn will join us, and you'll have a long journey to declare love to each other with the promise of treasure beyond comprehension."

Bella stopped pulling on the ties.

"You agree to remain quiet?"

She nodded, but before Jasper removed her gag, he warned, "Remember, if you scream or try to escape, I will kill him. If you cooperate, I will make this ship a temporary home for you."

She nodded again, and he removed the cloth from her mouth.

"Why did you have to kidnap me?" she whispered.

"I couldn't have you refuse my offer. A conversation with Quinn wouldn't benefit the situation. He's shy and unable to confess his true feelings." Jasper rubbed his hands. "I didn't know if he would have the courage to take the journey and bring you along despite my generous offer."

"He has more bravery than you know and has already protected me from many dangers." Bella's voice rose with each word, but no one would come to her aid. Not here. "I doubt he'll look at kidnapping me as a convincing way to trust you. He'll probably have you arrested instead."

"Having the nerve to fight physical battles is one thing, but it is quite different being able to tell a beautiful woman that he loves her." Jasper rubbed his chin. "I know he could have me arrested, but I don't think he will."

"How can you be sure?" she demanded.

"For the inverse of the reason you are being quiet," he touched his knife's hilt. "I will kill you if he reports my slight indiscretion of taking you by force." The captain smiled slowly. "I lied to you. I am a pirate, and this is how we get what we want, but even pirates can be civilized when people follow our will."

The rosy color left Bella's cheeks, and although her pallid face was still lovely, he'd rather see her earlier heated expression. Her fire was more appealing than her fearfulness.

Even though she was obviously terrified, Bella lifted her chin. "What is it that you need me to do?"

"Write him a letter. Beg him to join my crew and tell him you have already joined. Make the reason plausible, or I'll have to follow through with my threats."

Jasper whipped out his knife from his belt and placed it to her silky, white throat, which was too pretty to damage, but he knew he wouldn't have to. Fear filled her eyes.

Bella choked out, "I'll write the letter."

"Good. Now that nasty business is done. I will free your hands and feet, but don't try to escape. You'll find paper and quill on that desk over there for you to draft your letters."

"Letters? But if I only have to write to Quinn—"

"Send one to the de la Rose plantation explaining that you are leaving tonight for your new adventure."

Bella grimaced. "I'll miss tomorrow's wedding."

Jasper's mouth twitched. She was worried about a wedding? "Tell them I was in a hurry to leave. We've already spent more time in New Orleans than originally planned. I want to reach my destination before storm season. Just make it believable."

He untied Bella from the bed. She stood up shakily and rubbed her wrists, then walked to the desk with zero resistance.

She seemed to understand what was necessary to keep Quinn safe, but Jasper frowned. He hadn't realized how much the girl liked the hunched man until she bragged about his bravery. Her odd attraction to the monstrosity had surfaced when she took offense at the way Jasper mocked of Quinn's hump, but her current reactions revealed something more than a fleeting fancy.

Even though Bella's emotions would lead her to cooperate with him and save her beast, how deep were her feelings? Would they hinder his plans to gain her affection. Would the girl distract him from the imaginary mermaid during the long journey? Unlike the late Captain Starr, Jasper thought it bad form to force a woman to be his paramour. It was true he had taken her aboard his ship without her consent, but that was necessary knowing Quinn wouldn't be brave enough to join the crew. He assumed his superiority would eventually win Bella's affections, but perhaps he should have picked an easier target. Women were hard to decipher at best, and this girl was more bewildering than most.

He'd win, of course. The mystery of Bellarose had captured his attention in the first place, and he would unravel her, inch by inch.

Chapter 6

Bellarose

B ella's pounding heart might literally beat itself to death. Beads of sweat pooled behind her neck, and her stomach turned. Not only did reminders of her parents' death lingered among the briny odors of sea combined with the wet wood of the ship, but Quinn's life and her own were at stake.

Why did this cutthroat pirate want either of them? He was the scum of the earth and sea who took what he wanted and deserved none of it.

While Bella paced the room candlelight reflected off the shiny dark weathered wood desk. The captain's quarters matched the image Bella conjured up in her mind when she had read about them. Thick air with saltwater, leather, wood, and a faint scent of rum filled the area spacious as two of The Swan's rooms put together.

That's when she noticed the chair, storage chests, drawers and a four-poster bed all were of the same material. She brushed her fingers over the red velvet curtains that matched the bed coverlet, a bit of luxury in the rugged space. In the center of the room, charts, navigational tools, blank paper, a pen and quill and paper covered the desk.

She sat down at the writing table and her fingers nearly bent the quill before she had dipped it in the inkwell. Her mind scurried through words, and panic bubbled in her throat. How could she explain why she joined the crew? She couldn't hurt Quinn's feelings or propel him into doing something rash. No matter how she worded it, she had to lie, which was the last thing she wanted to do.

Captain Falcon—no, Jasper, because the scoundrel didn't deserve the title captain—tapped his foot. "What are you waiting for?" he whispered into her ear, "Write the letter—the hour is at hand."

His warm, spicy breath made her skin crawl, but she squared her shoulders.

"I'm not sure what will convince Quinn without hurting his feelings or making him suspicious that I'm being coerced."

"I already told him you were joining me to escape your life. I may have even alluded to the fact that you wanted to be rich again, and that if he wanted to give you the finer things life has to offer, he would join my crew." He pressed his index finger on the blank page. "I told him the best way to win your affections was to become wealthy, and you can confirm that here."

Bella's temples throbbed with heated anger.

Through clenched teeth she asked, "What other lies did you tell him about me?"

"I told him that you wanted the life you had before, and that if you choose him, I'll willingly give you up," the pirate said silkily. "If you can't decide between us, however, we'll duel for you at the end of the journey." Jasper straightened. "If I win, you'll stay with me, but if he wins, your journey will be complete. I will give up any claims I have on you."

"I'm not a piece of property you can barter over," Bella said, somehow keeping both anger and panic out of her voice.

"Perhaps. But I had to make it sound like you were willing to be my wife to escape your current life." He flashed her a toothy grin. "Quinn had to believe becoming part of my crew would give him a chance to change your mind."

"You cad!" Bella gripped the quill tighter. "I wouldn't choose to be with you even if you paid me all the jewels in the world!"

The pirate shrugged one powerful shoulder. "Ultimately, I'm going to win you over with my charms, and Quinn won't matter to you. You'll eventually admit that I'm the better man." He moved the blank sheet closer to her. "But for now, if you want to keep that boy alive, you will write what I tell you to write."

Bella stilled. "Why are you doing this?"

"I have my reasons."

"There are women who would probably beg to be at your beck and call for riches and a better life. Why pick me?"

"You're a challenge. They're not." He pointed to the paper. "Write the letter."

She steadied her shaking hand by gripping the quill even harder. No speck of good existed in a man who was encouraged by her resistance. He wasn't only a pirate; he was evil.

She would keep Quinn alive and find a way to beat Jasper at his own game if it was the last thing that she did. In the meantime, she painstakingly wrote the letter putting down the exact words he dictated, all the while hoping her obedience would appease his violent nature.

Dear Quinn,

I've decided to join Captain Falcon aboard his ship. Since I'm poor and don't belong at the plantation, Jasper has given me another option. I no longer want to be indebted to everyone, and this is my opportunity to change my fate.

He told me that he offered you the same thing, and I hope you decide to join us. We leave tonight at midnight, and I'm already on the ship.

Sincerely,

Bella

Then, Jasper forced her to write to Brooke and Antoine, though at least she was allowed to put it in her own words this time.

Dear Brooke and Antoine,

I hope you don't worry about me or find me ungrateful for all you've done for me, but I've decided to join Captain Falcon aboard his ship. He isn't a pirate as was rumored, so you needn't worry about my safety or virtue.

I am truly appreciative for all you have given me, but since I'm not family nor am I a servant at the plantation, I feel like an intruder. Once you are married, I will be useless to you both. I need to find my own way in this world, and Captain Falcon has given me that opportunity.

Plus, he offered Quinn a job aboard his ship, and without me, Quinn wouldn't come along. He needs to escape his father's cruelty, and we plan to make a life for ourselves.

Quinn hasn't proposed yet, but I know he will, and hopefully we can find a home in New Orleans when our journey is over.

I regret not being able to stay for your wedding, but we are leaving tonight, and there isn't time to say farewell. I hope to return someday and see your house full of happy children.

Sincerely,

Bella

Jasper's lips broadened as he reread Bella's letters.

He tromped to the door and yelled, "Sven!"

A short, older man appeared. "Captain?"

"Deliver this letter to Quinn, the stableboy and blacksmith at The Swan." He gave the man the letter. "Wait for him to read it, and if he agrees to join us, bring him back to the ship." Then he slipped Sven the second letter. "Give this to a mail courier in town to have delivered to Mr. de la Rose tomorrow." He lowered his voice, but Bella heard the words anyway. "I don't want them to try and talk Bella out of her decision."

Sven nodded and took the letters. "Yes, Captain."

The door shut, and Bella's hope for escape vanished when the captain again wrapped her wrists in rope, tied them to the bed, and left the room. If she hadn't been terrified before, she was now. She breathed in through her nose and out through her mouth to calm her ever-racing heart, but the stale smells inside the cabin made her choke. Tears rolled warmly down her cheeks.

How had she fallen for this? Of course, it had been too good to be true because the truth was, her life had been one misfortune after another. Whenever something good happened to her, it was only temporary. Even her life at the de la Rose plantation was impermanent. It might as well have been a dream. Quinn was the one bright light in her gloomy future, and because of this pirate's evil schemes, she was going to lose him forever.

In all the books she had read about villains and heroes, she'd never truly understood what was at stake until now. As she scrolled through the stories in her mind's eye, however, a beautiful library zoomed in and out of focus. Even her position changed. For a moment, she was curled up in a cozy chair in front of a warm fireplace, and the comforting scents of pine and cinnamon soothed her. Her tears stopped abruptly, but just when she was about to stand up and explore the magical place, the ropes burned her wrists and brought her back to reality.

She shook off the strange vision, which always returned whenever she recalled fairy tales with maidens in distress. Those poor young women were always rescued before they were ruined by the evil pirate or a wicked king, but this was the real world. Bella didn't have magic.

Where was the enchantress Aerowyn now?

If only she would appear and teach Captain Falcon a lesson with one of her spells and keep Quinn from falling into a trap.

Oh, how she wanted Quinn to join them—if that was a real possibility. He was her safe harbor. When she first arrived in New Orleans, he had led her to the job at The Swan, which provided room and board when she was penniless. When men made improper threats, Quinn interceded. His protection gave Bella courage to face anything. Before she admitted that she loved him, she wanted the chance to find out if he really loved her. Going back to the life of an aristocrat wasn't an option, but becoming a thief wasn't on her list of possible life changes either. Her stomach lurched at the thought of so much violence. Even if Quinn joined this crew, he wouldn't be able to save her. Falcon would kill him. To the depths of her soul, she wanted Quinn here, but Bella knew the truth.

With no one to help her, she would have to outwit this pirate and save herself.

Chapter 7

Aerowyn

Only a speck of sunlight reached through Ageless Isle's deep forest to creep inside the paned-glass window of Aerowyn's tree home. She yawned. Sleep had eluded her all night. Between the message sent to her through a magical link by her New Orlean's spy and Gerard's transmitted nightmares, she had been flooded with regrets about Bella and Gerard both, as well as, the other curses she had put on certain people. She flinched with each vivid reminder.

Stretching, she moved soundlessly from her floral bedspread, past Gerard's canine cushion, and into the kitchen to put the kettle on the stove. The tea would calm her agitated spirit and give her the energy she needed to tackle the day's tasks.

Ever since Gerard had entered her life, Aerowyn had begun to question her mission to rid the world of selfishness and evil and the methods she'd used. For every curse she cast, someone suffered before overcoming their sins to break the spell, and Gerard's emotions had niggled past her stoicism more times than she cared to admit.

The tea kettle whistled. She poured hot water over the strainer basket of loose leaves. The unique spice of the isle's tea filled her senses with a warming calm and pushed against her mixed emotions. Her fear and hopes for Gerard had nothing to do with King Peter's grand plan.

That hex the king had cast on Callista because she couldn't control his daughter, Isla, had greater implications than he had planned. In a round-about way, it was the very reason Aerowyn had to return to New Orleans to deal with a pirate whose life had been altered by the bitter decisions Callista had made after her curse.

Gerard's whimpers broke into her thoughts as they grew to a wretched whine. Aerowyn's grip tightened around the mug.

Poor Gerard. I'm sorry.

While he slept, he couldn't completely block her from his thoughts. He was stuck as her companion until he found a way to break the curse that had rebounded to him when it lifted from his brother. So, every night she watched him relive the days they met in the battleground hospital while she cared for his friend Leo. His dreams usually ended with her death, but this morning, the nightmare drew out past that as he relived his transformation into a wolf.

The next sip of Aerowyn's tea went down hard. She placed the cup down too quickly and liquid spilled onto the table. Her jaw tightened as his pain shot through her. Normally, she did nothing, even when he whimpered in his sleep or his legs twitched as if he ran, but this time, she had to. Not only for him. For what they must do.

Aerowyn crouched beside him and set her hand on his thick black fur. "Gerard?"

His head shot up, and his eyes flew open. Almost instantly, the images in her head vanished as he shut down the mental link.

"We're not in danger," she said soothingly.

He blinked.

She settled near his bed and smiled.

"King Peter, who is disguised as a human has messaged me through a mental link."

He yawned, then snapped his canine jaw shut. *And? Why did you wake me?*

"Do you remember when I told you we would eventually return to New Orleans?"

His voice sounded in her mind. *I remember. Are we going there now?*

"Yes. I need to intervene in another human's life. His name is Captain Jasper Falcon. He's a pirate who has no scruples to prevent him from doing whatever it takes to obtain his desires. Jasper needs to be taught a lesson."

She reached for her tea and stared at it.

So?

"Not only has Falcon ruined many lives through larceny and murder, but he's about to hurt someone you love like a sister."

Gerard gave a low growl.

Bella or Brooke?

"Brooke is safe. She will marry your brother Antoine soon. It's Bella."

His fur raised on end. *I thought Quinn was Bella's protector.*

"He was, but unfortunately, he's unable to do what's necessary to keep Bella away from the pirate captain. King Peter is on the ship in a disguise, but I don't know why. He might be there for another reason." Aerowyn swallowed hard. "He never fills me in on his plans until it's absolutely necessary, but we need Bella to be safe."

Gerard barked. *I'm well aware of your lessons. This Jasper character doesn't stand a chance.*

"I haven't decided yet what I will do to him. It depends on what King Peter has planned."

He narrowed his eyes. *Why does King Peter need Bella?*

She sensed Gerard was suspicious, and Aerowyn couldn't blame him. She couldn't tell him that he, too, was part of the king's plans. Frankly, she didn't understand that, either. "I'm not completely sure, but I'll find out before I cast more curses. I can see that Jasper has a path for either redemption or ruin, and Bella isn't going to be his salvation."

Gerard stood and shook himself. *Right. Let's go.*

Aerowyn finished her tea and pulled out the golden scepter with a sun-shaped design at the tip. She swirled the wand, and her home faded away into complete darkness, then into uneven docks and tall ships. In a flash, the warmth of Ageless Isle was replaced with a damp chill of the night on Port of New Orleans.

Chapter 8

Jasper

J asper locked his cabin door and jogged after his first mate. "Sven!"

The older man pivoted toward him. "Captain?"

"Don't take that letter to Quinn."

"Sir?"

Jasper forced a chuckle. "I only had her write to Quinn to pacify Bella. The boy turned down my offer, and the letter won't change his mind."

Sven raised one eyebrow. "Did you really want it to change his mind?"

"Bah! That's none of your concern." Jasper ground his teeth. He didn't know for sure, but he wasn't going to give Quinn any more chances. "The letter going to Antoine de la Rose, however, must be delivered. He'll notice Bella's absence and has the means to send someone to rescue her."

"Ah," Sven said. "But only if they suspect foul play?"

"Exactly." He handed Sven a bag of gold coins and lowered his voice. "I want Quinn dead to prevent Antoine from discovering the truth. The letter says Quinn has joined our crew. I know you're opposed to harming others so use these coins to hire someone to kill him and dump his ugly body in the swamps where no one will ever find it."

Sven took the coins hesitantly. "Isn't there another way to deal with Quinn?"

"No. Obey or suffer the consequences." Jasper palmed the sword at his side. "And while you're in town, gather the men. We sail tonight. Also, pay someone to deliver Bella's note to Rose Manor after we leave."

"Aye aye, Captain," the first mate said, then shuffled off the ship.

Alone on the deck in the moonlight, Jasper pulled out the finely crafted sword Quinn had made him. It was a shame he wouldn't be making any more. This one was magnificent. Jasper grinned.

And so, I end up with two of Quinn's prizes.

Unfamiliar footsteps pulled his attention to the gangplank, and he startled, his hand tightening on the sword's grip. An old woman with an abnormally black wolf-like dog stood amidship.

Jasper scowled. "You don't belong here."

The woman leaned heavily on a walking stick. "I beg of you, Captain, let me be part of your journey."

Unexplained sweat beaded on his neck, and he shivered as if non-existent spiders crawled up his back. Something was wrong.

Jasper lifted his sword. "You need to leave now, or I'll force you."

She pushed back her hood. Maybe the woman wasn't as old as he'd originally thought because her raven locks only had occasional stripes of white, and her face wasn't wrinkled. The gold pendant around her neck would make a prosperous trade for many things, but her unnerving, violet stare kept him at bay.

The gigantic dog's human-like eyes gave Jasper the odd feeling the creature was judging him.

A potent vapor of spice and musk enveloped Jasper, and light-headedness almost toppled him from his feet.

He shook off the drunken feeling. "We can't have you or a dog on a long journey."

"I can help you navigate."

"I don't think so," he scoffed.

"Ageless Isle." She whispered a harmony of letters blended like a breeze.

Goosebumps formed on Jasper's arms. She must have him under a spell. He swallowed.

"How do you know where I'm going?"

Suddenly seeming even younger than before, she smiled. "You have told others you were going to Ageless Isle. There is only one island with that name."

"This ship isn't for passengers," he protested.

The enigmatic lady transformed into a young maiden with long golden hair. Her eyes remained violet, but her walking stick became a golden scepter topped with a sun-shaped design.

Jasper couldn't blink. "Blimey."

"I'm Aerowyn, the enchantress." Her voice was melodic. "I've come here to warn you."

"Ab-b-bout what?" Jasper stammered.

"You must discontinue your pirate ways."

Her words brought him back to his senses. Ignoring the dripping sweat and crawling skin, Jasper flexed his muscular frame and straightened his shoulders.

"Who are you to threaten me? You're such a slight thing. I could overpower you in a heartbeat."

"Not all threats are physical. Don't dismiss my abilities because of my size."

Her beautiful voice and face were a ridiculous contrast to her words. He laughed out loud as he summed up the enchanting creature before him. He really should stop the consumption of so much rum—the best explanation for Aerowyn's drastic change in appearance—but he was no longer afraid.

"Your looks are too beguiling, and I can't summon up the ability to fear you no matter what you say."

"Fear me or not. I'm only here to warn you that if you succeed in your plan to kidnap and spoil Bellarose's virtue, you will be cursed." She patted the dog's head. "Ask Gerard here about how my spells work."

Jasper smirked. "Am I supposed to know who Gerard is?"

"I know you've heard tales of his heroics at The Swan. Gustave told you Bella was fired for her mistreatment of him."

"Do you really expect me to believe you turned a man into an animal because of bad behavior? What did he do? Get too frisky with you?" He leered at her. "I wouldn't blame him for trying."

The creature growled, but this was Jasper's ship, *He* was the terror of the ocean, not this mangy dog. His sword in his hand, Jasper edged closer to Aerowyn where he could stab the dog or woman before either of them knew what had happened.

She glanced at the dog, then back. "You should be careful."

"I should be careful? Don't you know I'm a dangerous pirate? I could overpower you easily."

The dog named Gerard snarled.

"No, you can't hurt me." She held up her palm. "Stop moving before you regret your actions."

"My motto is 'no regrets and never look back.' I never have remorse over anything I choose to do willingly."

Gerard flashed sharp-looking teeth.

"It's your risk, not mine."

Jasper grabbed at Aerowyn, but the wolf-dog lunged. In one bite, it chomped off Jasper's left hand before he could touch her.

A shriek tore from Jasper's throat, and crimson spurted. Jasper's sword clanked to the floorboards as he dropped to his knees. The coppery smell of his own blood twisted his stomach. His energy drained away, just as his blood did. Jasper dropped onto the planks.

Through the ringing in his ears, Jasper could hear Aerowyn singing. The strange tune swelled. His vision cleared, and his wound knitted together as if cauterized by hot iron. Aerowyn waved her wand. His separated hand moved from the deck to her palm. Jasper gawked, then used his good arm to push himself to his knees.

Her song stopped. "You didn't drink too much rum, Captain. You only underestimated Gerard's protective nature. You threatened to harm me, so he stopped you. However rashly he acted, it is a warning." She raised the wand. "And this is a demonstration of my capabilities."

Before Jasper's eyes, a silver hook suddenly replaced his missing body part. He gulped and staggered to his feet. His hand... gone? Replaced by curving metal? Horror and anger battled in his heart, and anger won. He gestured at the gruesome appendage in her hand.

"Give back my hand, you witch!"

Aerowyn remained calm. "No."

Disbelief and revulsion engulfed him. "What are you going to do with it?"

"I will keep it until you change your path. Remember, I gave you the hook out of generosity. I understand that a sailor needs his hands. It will be a reminder of what we have discussed and prevent you from harming Bella."

"You can return it?" Jasper held up the hook. "I will get my hand back?"

"That depends entirely up to you. Your choices from now on will determine whether the hook is a permanent fixture. Your own actions will dictate whether I curse you forever or not."

He opened his mouth to protest, but before he could make any more demands, Aerowyn and her animal companion evaporated like fog.

"Give me back my hand!"

But his scream for his severed hand was futile.

Jasper grabbed the hook with his other arm and strained to pull it off, but it stayed in place. Panting, he dropped to his knees on the red-stained deck. Fury built inside him like a storm.

His breathing calmed and the vehemence transitioned to resolve. That witch couldn't be everywhere and she wouldn't be able to see how he treated Bella. He'd accept the hooked hand for now. Once he entered the open seas, she wouldn't be able to find him. When the *Black Fear* was in the middle of the ocean, he would evade the enchantress and her wolf and still be able to take advantage of Bella to spite the enchantress's warnings.

Jasper clenched his one hand into a fist. This ship was his escape from those who wanted to dictate how he should live his life. He hadn't gone through torture and risk to have the control wrested away from him.

When he couldn't have safety for his crew and himself, he killed Captain Starr. When he couldn't have his dream girl, the fictional mermaid, he kidnapped Bella.

Nothing was going to come between Captain Jasper Falcon and his desires.

Nothing.

Chapter 9

Bellarose

Bella pulled against the ropes in an attempt to escape the pirate captain's bed posts and her wrists grew raw. For a brief moment, fear lessened when she recalled Quinn's confession to Jasper. He loved her. He would come to her rescue once he joined the crew and discovered things weren't as the captain said they would be.

But at that thought, her mood plummeted. The captain was a liar. Maybe Quinn's reported confession was a falsehood. Maybe the pirate had invented that story to lure her away from the plantation and kidnap her since he had known she intended to talk to Quinn before accepting the offer.

She redoubled her efforts, and the hemp rope burned her skin.

Outside the cabin, the sounds of activity grew. Boards creaked, and water slapped the sides of the ship. Scurrying feet and hoarse shouts made it obvious the ship was leaving port.

Where is Quinn?

He wouldn't have wasted any time after receiving her letter, or at least that was what she hoped. The captain couldn't keep her tied up after Quinn arrived. If Jasper didn't allow them to leave, which she was beginning to suspect was the case, she had every confidence that Quinn would be able to win in a sword fight against the pirate.

Through the large window at the stern of the captain's quarters, the moonlight rippled on the water. The darker the sky grew, the darker Bella's mood became. Doubts crept into her mind.

Maybe Quinnn hates me now that he thinks I'm only interested in money.

Her thoughts raced. Would Quinn, who had been ridiculed all his life, assume Bella was shallow enough to be swayed by a ruggedly handsome and prosperous captain?

What would Quinn, who had always protected her virtue, think of her now if he believed she had thrown it all away the first chance she had to return to the life she had in France?

And what was worse? Quinn not really loving her, or having his opinion of her marred by lies? If he could believe such horrendous untruths about her, then maybe he wasn't the man she thought he was. Her cowardly father should have shielded her from life's harsh realities, but he didn't. Why did she expect more from Quinn?

Bile rose into her throat.

Does Quinn actually believe I'd marry Captain Falcon?

Hot tears drenched Bella's cheeks. She tried to wipe them on her shoulder but couldn't reach with her arms tied to the bedposts.

Her nose dripped, and disgust joined her kaleidoscope of emotions.

Finally, her sobs subdued. Hiccups followed.

She wrestled her feelings under control. Emotions were awful traitors. They would reveal weakness—something Bella couldn't allow Jasper to see.

The ship's movement changed, and she turned her head to watch Port New Orleans disappear out the stern windows. The bed jiggled, and loose objects on Jasper's desk rolled around. A woody must scent replaced the smells of land and port, and the crew's ditties about mermaids and treasure rose above the sounds of water slapping the ship. Moonlight shined brightly over the wake she could see through the captain's window.

Whether it was the cheery song or something else that turned her thoughts, Bella's books and stories came to mind. Perhaps she needed to rescue herself? In *The Scorned Fae*, the princess rather than the prince conquered the villain.

Bella squared her jaw and squirmed into a seated position. She was going to stop wallowing in tears, sniffed—though a handkerchief would have been preferable—and become the hero of her own story. A few more tears fell, but she swallowed hard and fought back any rogue drops.

"I can escape Jasper." She whispered the promise to herself as steps thundered toward the cabin. "I will figure out his weakness. Gerard couldn't conquer me, and neither will that dastardly pirate."

A key turned in the lock, and Jasper entered the room. "Based on your tear-stained face, you must know Quinn hasn't joined us."

"Yes." Bella held her head high. She couldn't afford to let the captain know that without Quinn at her side, she feared Jasper Falcon even more.

"I'm sorry Quinn wasn't the man you thought he was." The captain tut-tutted. "I thought he would have joined my crew to escape his awful father even if he had no desire to win your affections." Jasper pulled a handkerchief from his breast pocket and wiped Bella's cheeks.

She tried to pull away unsuccessfully.

"Quinn really isn't a very smart person for letting a treasure like you go."

"My wrists are quite sore," she said, unwilling to give him the privilege of an answer. "Is there any reason to keep me tied here any longer?"

"Oh my, I forgot all about that. Of course you don't need to be bound any more. You won't want to escape by water unless you wish to die. I know there are alligators in the Mississippi River." He paused and then added, "It seems you must remain aboard my ship and make the best of the situation."

Jasper's lips turned upward, but the expression didn't reach his eyes. When he went to untie her bindings, however, he tried to loosen the knots of the ropes with only one hand.

A silver hook glinted on his other arm. Bella blinked. "Didn't you have both hands earlier today?"

He cursed, then clenched his jaw.

Is that dried blood stains on his sleeve?

Cut off?

She stared at the hook. "Do I dare ask what happened since the last time I saw you?"

"A hag's dog bit it off," he snapped.

"A hag's dog," she repeated slowly. *A black wolf?*

"She transformed into a witch, used some kind of hex to seal the wound, and give me this thing." Jasper lifted his left arm, and the hook gleamed in the moonlight.

Bella's stomach lurched.

"Aerowyn and Gerard!"

His eyes narrowed with suspicion. "How do you know them?"

"She is the one who cursed everyone who lived at the de la Rose plantation." Bella swallowed hard. "Antoine transformed into a wolf every day and only stayed human for a short time before the sun set, but Gerard, his brother, took the curse upon himself. Now Gerard is a wolf, though he doesn't get to change as Antoine did. I honestly thought they had gone back to her island."

"I didn't believe in magic or curses until today." He scowled and lifted his new accessory. "When she first threatened me, I didn't take her seriously. You can see where that got me."

"Aerowyn is a cunning enchantress. I don't trust her," Bella said aloud.

Is she the reason I'm on this ship?

Why didn't Aerowyn stay and help her? Bella didn't like the enchantress. who played with people's lives, but she wanted to see Gerard. Was he safe? Bella had been so angry at him, but deep down, Gerard was a broken-hearted man who hadn't really meant her harm. In fact, compared to Jasper, he was a gentleman.

Bella dared to ask, "What did she say?"

"None of your business." Jasper's eyes darkened. "We're far away from her now, and even a powerful enchantress must have limitations."

Quinn wasn't onboard, but maybe fear of Aerowyn could keep the captain and his men in line? Bella had to take the chance.

"I wouldn't be so confident you're too far from her reach. I've seen her disguise her appearance. At this moment, she could be a member of your crew."

Jasper clunked his hook onto the bedside table. "Bah! That's ridiculous!"

Bella shifted as far away from Jasper as her captive state allowed. "Since you aren't going to be able to loosen these tight knots," she said cautiously, "maybe you should ask one of your crew to help?"

Jasper's brows puckered. "I'll ask Sven."

He left, and Bella fidgeted nervously in her bindings. He was right about her chances of escape. There was no way off the ship while it sailed. A shudder ran down her spine. She didn't even want to think about what plans he had for her.

The door opened, and a stout man with gray hair entered and bowed gracefully to her.

"Bonjour," he said softly with genuine French intonation. "I'm sorry for the captain's behavior."

Puzzled, Bella stared at the older man. His speech and mannerisms were too refined, and quite unlike the other pirates she overheard.

"You aren't like him at all, are you?"

His pleasant face almost put her at ease.

"Not really."

"Then... how did *you* end up on this ship of pirates?"

"You wouldn't believe me if I told you."

Jasper strode into the room, and his voice cracked through their conversation. "Sven, untie the ropes. Bella doesn't need to hear your life's story."

"Yes, Captain," Sven said.

He glanced at her and gave a cautious smile, but his hands shook while he worked on the ropes. A gold pendant with a diamond dangled from his neck as he leaned to untie her other hand. Something about it was familiar to Bella, but trying to figure out how was forgotten when he whispered, "I promise you'll be okay." Then he winked as if he knew something she didn't.

The bindings fell. Bella scooted off the bed and stood on the opposite side.

The captain growled, "That will be all. Go see to the crew and make sure they are making haste to get far from New Orleans."

As Sven scurried away, Jasper gave Bella what he must have meant to be a seductive grin. "We're alone once again. What should we do first?"

Bella inched away from him. "I think I better sleep somewhere other than here. I know you promised me your room, but I can stay on deck under the stars."

His leer faded. "That would be bad form on my part to kick you out of my bed. Of course you will stay here. I will be glad to use Sven's cabin, but—" he sidled closer "—if you really feel guilty about keeping me from my quarters, we could share the space. It's big enough for two."

Bella felt the color drain from her face. "I'll never be your mistress, Captain Falcon."

She slapped her hand over her mouth.

"This will be a long journey, let's not be formal with each other. Please call me Jasper." His eyes crinkled in the corners. "And, dear Bella, I wouldn't think of sullying your virtue. You have such a low opinion of me."

Bella rubbed her sore wrists. "Based on the fact that you've kidnapped me, I think my judgement of you is accurate."

"It's true I took you without your consent, and if you were just any wench, I would have done worse with you, but..." Jasper's attention jerked from her to the stern's window.

Bella followed his gaze. Behind the ship in the churning water under the silvery moonlight, something popped out directly in the lighted path.

"What was that?"

Jasper moved to face Bella. He drummed his fingers on his side. "Bah! The Mississippi has all kinds of curious creatures." He neared Bella. She backed into the bed but remained standing. "I'll be honest. I've never kidnapped a lady before, but I needed to be distracted from things that haunt my dreams."

Bella believed his sincerity despite her distrust of the man. Now she felt pity and fear for Jasper, which only complicated her emotions.

He continued, "I'm no fool. I know if I force myself onto you, it won't end well for either of us." Jasper's sinister expression returned. "We'll have a much more pleasant voyage if you choose my attention freely, which you will, soon enough."

Bella's hands fisted. *Over my dead body.*

He moved to the wardrobe in the corner. His hook clanked against the latch. He must have forgotten about it. Jasper growled, opened the cabinet single handedly, and pulled out some clothes.

"I need to change out of this bloody shirt."

Bella's face warmed.

He struggled with his buttons and before giving up. His face puckered. "Bah! I'll be back to see how you're doing in the morning."

Jasper draped the clothing over his arm, managed to open the door, and slammed it behind him. She heard a click so she rushed to check the knob. The door was locked from the outside.

Bella sagged back onto the bed. At least he didn't undress in front of her.

Odd, though after they had seen the unknown object in the water, Jasper seemed unfocused. Was that mysterious thing part of the nightmares he mentioned? Not that it mattered, but she did understand haunting dreams. Even with a slight tinge of empathy for the man, she wasn't going to be used as a diversion from his night terrors.

As soon as she found someone to help her, Bella was going to escape the *Black Fear.*

Chapter 10

Jasper

Jasper headed to Sven's quarters with his clothes bunched up in his arms. He wanted out of the bloody shirt, but his mind was muddled with that image he saw in the river. When he passed Jeb, who gawked at his new appendage, the man's expression only reminded him of how things hadn't gone as perfectly as he had planned.

"What are you staring at?" Jasper snapped.

"Cap'n, what happ'n to yer hand?"

"A witch took it and gave me this hook." Jasper struggled with the clothes hanging from his arms. "Here, take these to Sven's cabin. I'll be staying there from now on."

Jeb took the items. "Is the witch stay'n in yer room?"

"No." Jasper growled. "I'll explain everything to the crew in the morning, but for now, no more questions."

"Yes sir," Jeb said then left Jasper alone.

Still wearing stained clothes, Jasper stomped up to the poop deck. Not because he was secretly hoping to see what he had noticed through his cabin window would appear again. No, Bella was supposed to divert him from obsessing over the red-haired mermaid from his dreams.

Although... Bella's unwillingness to share his room was a sign she wasn't going to be as easy to win over as he had planned.

That girl wasn't going to be scared into giving him what he wanted, and a frightened female would be neither sincere nor enthusiastic. Besides, he wasn't a desperate coward who had to force young women to bend to his whims. He might have a hook for a left hand, but he knew how women admired him. He only needed a different tactic. He needed her to stroke his ego.

Jasper tapped the fingers of his right hand on the rail. She'd hoped for her misshapen hero to rescue her, so perhaps the way to her heart was to channel Quinn's behavior. He scowled. Groveling was foreign to him.

Bella might have a strong will, but he would wear her down. In the end. She'd fall for him and forget the pathetic man who was probably already being eaten by alligators in the swamp.

Despite his better judgement, Jasper's eyes searched the foam in the *Black Fear's* wake.

Of course there was no mermaid looking up at him, her fire-bright hair washed to silver by the moonlight. The faded memory of a young mergirl wiping his tears after his mother had beaten him were nothing but a foolish boy's imagination.

Mermaids were myths that had no use in real life.

Jasper turned away from the dark water and stomped to Sven's cabin to change his bloody shirt and steal some sleep.

Chapter 11

Bellarose

The first night on the *Black Fear*, Bella tossed and turned in bed with sweat-drenched clothes. While she had resisted sobbing in front of Jasper, when alone, tears broke free once again. Nightmarish images of the horrific journey across the Atlantic haunted her. Even though Jasper's room smelled of leather and wood, memories of vomit and human waste were so vivid she could smell them. After the horrific journey that led to her parents' untimely deaths, she had promised herself she would never set foot on a ship again. Yet here she was, on a pirate vessel.

"Never say never," Bella whispered.

Sunlight eventually brightened the room. Bella eased out of bed and met her puffy-eyed reflection in the standing mirror near the armoire.

She rubbed her throbbing temple. Crying always gave her a headache.

Bella sponged off the night's perspiration with the water in the wash basin and searched the chest at the end of the bed for something clean to wear.

If I work alongside the men, maybe I can gain some allies against Jasper.

She shook her head at the absurd thought of pirates defending her against their captain, but maybe Sven would help. He'd seemed sympathetic to her plight.

She found brown breeches and held them up for size. They were a little baggy, but she cinched a belt around her waist, then slipped a loose-fitting shirt over her head and tucked it into the pants.

Despite her restless night, she was determined to escape Jasper's clutches. She'd ward off any of his advances. Maybe Quinn's self-defense lessons would come in handy. Her heart sank at the thought of her friend, but she straightened her shoulders.

A quiet click pulled her suddenly panicked attention to the door, but when no one entered, Bella's racing heart calmed. She needed to get out of the claustrophobic cabin. She tried the knob. It was unlocked. The anxiety returned. When did the door get unlocked? Was that the noise she had heard a second ago? Anyone could have entered the cabin during the night, but they hadn't. She needed to get her emotions under control. A crisp ocean breeze would clear her head and she had to think rationally to charter this new course her life had taken.

Bella exited the chamber, and after some wrong turns, she reached the upper deck where several men swabbed the planks and hoisted the sails. They stopped what they were doing to gawk at her, and she immediately regretted her decision to seek fresh air.

From behind her Jasper spoke, "Men!"

Bella spun around, and her cheeks warmed. Jasper was shirtless. The only other time she'd seen a half-naked man was when Antoine had transformed from a wolf.

"As I explained to you earlier this morning, not only did a witch give me this hook, but this lass—" he pointed to her with his hook "—Bella Bonnay, has joined our crew from New Orleans."

The crew buzzed with murmurs.

"Havin' a girl onboard is bad luck."

"She's pretty."

Jasper raised his voice above the noise. "Please treat her as a welcome guest of mine." He paused, and his gaze skimmed over her clothing. "Despite her... attire, she won't be required to carry her own weight but is allowed to do whatever she chooses."

She knew she should look away but his hook, intricate tattoos, and sun-kissed skin fascinated her. Of course he caught her gawking. He waggled his eyebrows, and she darted her gaze to the ocean. He probably thought she was attracted to him.

That wasn't it, though. It was the ink itself that drew her attention. Still, she turned her back to squash her curiosity and face the front of the ship. A deep breath calmed her jittery nerves while she took in the beautiful, azure sea. The sun was fully up, casting light into the transparent water.

"Good morning, my lady."

Bella startled and glanced back.

Jasper wiped his moistened chest with a soft cloth and donned a pristine white shirt, sliding the loose cuff over his hook. "Are you feeling well? Your face is flushed." His eyes roamed over her body. "I wore those when I was a young lad. They look good on you."

Bella forced herself to face forward again. "Yes, I'm fine despite the circumstances. The sun is warmer than I expect for this time of year."

"We're heading to a part of the world with different seasons than New Orleans. Maybe I should find you a parasol to shade your tender skin?" His gaze lingered too long below her neckline. "Rumors say that Ageless Isle remains the same perfect season all year long. Magic supposedly has something to do with the weather. In fact, I believe we've been assisted with a little of that magic already."

"Why do you say that?"

"We should still be on the Mississippi River, but during the night we sailed into the ocean. We shouldn't have reached the sea for another three days."

Bella studied his expression to see if he was jesting with her, but there were lines etched across his forehead.

"I guess it is easier to believe in magic now that you've experienced it firsthand—I mean for yourself." She bit her bottom lip over the 'hand' reference.

"Ahem," he muttered. "How did you sleep?"

"Horribly. My previous voyage on a ship was awful, and last night brought back the memory."

Jasper frowned. "I know your parents died on a ship. Is that the bad memory you speak of?" Then his eyes roamed her body again. "The offer to share the room with you is still on the table. I could distract you from those nightmares."

"No, thank you," she said curtly.

"You're acting tame today. I expected more fight with my offer."

She clenched her fists. "I'm tired, and you threatened both my life and Quinn's! To top things off, I have a headache."

He stared at her thoughtfully for a few minutes. "Perhaps I could get Sven to fetch you some of his herbal remedies for pain. He's the ship's physician among some of his other duties."

"That explains why he doesn't act like a pirate."

"Well, please don't hold my occupation against me." He winked. "I'm a very refined pirate and not like the nasty tales one reads about in books."

Given his threats, murder and larceny were probably part of his regular routine, but wisdom kept her from asking how either of those things could be done with refinement. She rubbed her temples again.

"I think I will accept Sven's remedy for my pain."

"Sven, please come assist Bella," Jasper bellowed, and she winced at the noise.

Sven was upon them in an instant.

He dipped his head toward Bella.

"Aye, Captain. What can I do for her?"

"My lady has a headache. I told her you had remedies for such maladies."

Sven smiled, and his rich brown eyes crinkled around the corners. Once again, she felt safer in his presence.

"I have some herbs that will help, but I'll steep some tea to make them go down smoother." He turned to leave, but then added, "Miss Bella, if you don't mind, I'll meet you in the captain's cabin with the medicine."

"That will be perfect."

She navigated her way back to the captain's quarters and sat down on the bed. The pounding in her head put her in a foul mood. It was only day one of her captivity, but she was already tired of it. She hated the way Jasper eyed her. She loathed that she was trapped on a moving prison. And most of all, Bella was broken hearted that Quinn didn't come for her.

Nevertheless, she'd find allies after her pain was gone and she'd make Jasper regret he ever looked at her.

Chapter 12

Jasper

Jasper watched Bella wander back to the cabin, and work was forgotten. Scowling, he paced the upper deck.

The fact that she cared for the misshapen young man's life and rejected Jasper was bewildering. Not only was he much more handsome, he could offer her riches, security, and respect. All Quinn could give her was a life of scorn and suffering. He was better than Quinn in every way, but Jasper needed to convince Bella of that fact.

He wasn't going to be able to persuade her here. It had been a few hours since she had left him and Sven's remedy had probably started to work. Perhaps she would be more receptive to him with her headache gone. Jasper wasn't known for his patience and he hadn't formed a plan. Besides, a captain shouldn't have to wait.

He jogged to his quarters and knocked on the door.

"Who is it?"

Her voice was groggy.

"It's Jasper. I wanted to ensure Sven took good care of you."

Feet shuffled, and the door swung open. She blinked up at him with puffy eyes. Her mussed hair hung down her shoulders.

"I'm sorry. Were you sleeping?"

She yawned. "Yes." She stiffened and backed away. "Remember? I said I hadn't slept well last night."

Jasper eyed her attire. "Of all the clothes you could have chosen from my trunk, I didn't expect you to pick what I wore as a cabin boy."

"These are more practical." She tied back her loose hair. "I know you said I didn't need to help out with duties aboard ship, but I don't want to be useless. I felt the need to dress the part, but I probably need a smaller size."

"My dear Bella, your beauty will be useful enough for morale. Now, if you prefer wearing a man's clothes, I can ask our ship's tailor to make something that fits you better."

She perked up slightly. "You have a tailor?"

He shrugged one shoulder. "One of my men was a tailor before he joined the *Black Fear*." Jasper walked further into the room and Bella increased the distance between them. "Perhaps I could ask him to sew you something if you agree to have dinner with me."

Her eyes darted between the old blade leaning against the wall and him. "I will have to eventually eat, but I prefer not to eat alone with you."

He held back what he wanted to really say.

"Nonetheless, I will ask the tailor to help with your attire."

Bella exhaled. "Then all I have left to do is find someone who will practice crossing blades with me."

Jasper pushed the memory of Starr falling into the ocean aside and forced a grin. "Don't be getting any ideas in that pretty little head. My men won't allow you to kill me, if that's what you're planning." For a second, he saw her with a sword in her hand, next to Quinn. It wouldn't do to have her thinking of that man, so he stretched his grin wider and added, "Is there anything else I can do for you?"

He stepped in front of Bella so she would have to look into his eyes. He was told they were one of his best features to woo a woman into trusting him.

"No. Now that my headache is subsiding, I want to catch up on lost sleep."

He brushed a hair from her face and she flinched. "Tut, tut, you are a nervous girl."

He didn't feel anything for the attractive Bella, but he thought she could keep his imaginary mermaid away, so he asked, "Maybe I could read you a story to help you fall asleep?"

She backed away from him. "No thank you."

"I could sing you a lullaby." He gave her what he thought was a swarthy smile. "I could figure out something to wear you out."

Bella stumbled back against the trunk at the foot of his bed. "You cad!"

She quickly steadied her footing. While Jasper knew he wasn't imitating Quinn's behavior as he should have done, at least now she wasn't thinking about the deformed black-smith. He'd wear her inhibitions down eventually, but not today.

"I'm only jesting." He winked. "I'll leave you the key. Lock the door if that will make you feel totally safe. I told the men not to touch you, but they are pirates."

He held out the key for Bella, and she closed in enough distance to take it. Her ruby lips caught his attention, and the sudden desire to pull her in for a long kiss, thus to erasing all thoughts of Quinn swept over him, but the timing wasn't right. If Aerowyn and her beast hadn't taken away his hand, perhaps he wouldn't allow such things to hinder him, but his hook took away some of his debonair tactics.

Turning quickly, he left and shut the door behind him. The patter of feet, a faint scrape, and then a soft metallic click assured Jasper she was locked away from the crew and himself

It wasn't until late afternoon that Bella emerged onto the upper deck, still wearing the loose-fitting men's clothing, with her hair tied back in a ribbon. Since today he wasn't going to seduce the fair maiden, he'd have some of the other men help her fit in aboard the ship while he attended to his duties.

Jasper made a shallow bow. "How are you feeling?"

She blushed prettily. "Much better."

"I made sure the men kept racket to a minimum. I didn't want anyone to disturb your sleep."

"Thank you. I do feel better. I am ready to make myself useful." She straightened her shoulders and looked him square in the eye. "I will be a part of the crew and nothing else."

He lifted a brow. "Whatever do you mean?"

"You know exactly what I mean," she snapped.

Jasper chortled. "Well, I thought you may like me more than you let on. I caught you staring at me when I was shirtless, but I didn't let it go to my head." He almost rubbed his chin with his hook and abruptly dropped his arm. "You'll have to get accustomed to various forms of undress around all these men." Before she could rant about that, Jasper changed the subject. "Let me introduce you to our ship's tailor. The journey will be more enjoyable if you're comfortable."

Bella narrowed her eyes. "I doubt you care about my comfort."

There she went again assuming the worst about him. Not that she was completely wrong, though, he had no regrets, but she needed to think better of him if he was going to gain her trust.

"Follow me." He motioned with his hook. "I think Jeb is in the galley. Most of us have already eaten, but you can have your meal. Then Jeb can take your measurements."

He whistled for Sven, who fell into step behind him. Bella followed them down a ladder and toward the galley.

The smell of beef broth lingered in the air, and Jasper was thankful it masked the body odor and other foul smells of the ship. He couldn't woo her into his arms if she was nauseous.

Jeb sat at a table with Will and a few other men, who were cussing up a storm. Jasper cleared his throat loudly.

"Men, please watch your language when Bella is around."

They gawked. If they were thinking indecent thoughts, he didn't care, as long as they kept their hands to themselves. Bella was his.

"Aye, Captain," a few chorused.

"Jeb, Bella chose men clothes over the fancy dresses we acquired on our last... trade."

Jeb smirked.

"You're the best tailor," Jasper continued. "If she prefers to wear trousers, then I know you can make that happen. Don't let me down." He glared fiercely at the men. "No one touches her without permission, and Sven will be nearby to enforce that rule. You hear?"

"Aye, Captain," the men replied in unison.

"Mind your table manners," Jasper motioned to the remaining food. "And get her something to eat."

Jeb jumped to his feet, grabbed a plate, and dished up biscuits and stew for Bella. When he plunked grog and slopped it in front of her, it splashed on her hand. Jasper glared at Jeb.

"I trust you will be gentlemen." Jasper caught Sven's eye as he turned.

The first mate nodded.

Then, Jasper left Bella to fend for herself.

As he exited the galley, he overheard Bella say, "Thank you, Jeb."

He couldn't spend his whole day watching over Bella. Despite a whispering doubt, he climbed the steps to the stern. He had a ship to run.

Chapter 13

Bellarose

The other pirates weren't as well-groomed as Jasper. The stench of body odor covered the scent of stew, but what was worse was the way their eyes crawled up and down her like insects.

She drew a deep breath then said, as sunnily as she could, "Where did you learn to be a tailor, Jeb?"

He raked dirty fingers through his ginger hair. "Me mum, mos'ly, before I joined the crew. She made clothes for fancy ladies."

Bella turned to the greasy-haired lad beside Jeb. He seemed a few years younger than the tailor, but he was old enough that his stare made Bella uncomfortable. "What's your name?"

"I'm Will." He puffed out his chest. "I'm the best one to ask if you want somethin' special from the cook since I'm his friend."

Bella dipped her head. "That's good to know."

Sven chimed in, "These lads are as trustworthy as you can get aboard a ship full of pirates."

The two grinned at this implication that they were the best aboard the ship.

They sat up straighter and stopped leering at her. Sven had the men's obvious respect, and Bella took note of it. With these three men for allies, she might survive after all.

She swallowed hard. "I know there are women's dresses for me to wear, but I want practical clothes. It'll be easier for me to contribute as a crew member.

"You won't be needed in that capacity," Sven said, "but perhaps Jeb can use your help with repairing the men's clothes."

Instead of agreeing with the first mate, however, Jeb looked at Bella's plate. "Ye ain't touched yer food. Do ye wan somefing else before I get yer measurements?"

She chuckled nervously and took a bite of beef. Her lips turned upward. "Delicious."

Will beamed. "I helped prepare that wif Finn, who is the cook."

Bella ate the surprisingly tasty food until her dishes were empty. A full stomach did feel better.

"Thank you for feeding me." She placed the stew spoon onto the table. "Now I'm ready to dress like a pirate."

"Righ'." Jeb pushed away from the bench. "Bella, come wif me. I'll take ye to me sewin' room. Sven, she'll be safe wif me, if ye have fings to do."

Sven stood. "Very well. Don't do anything the captain would consider bad form."

Will stayed to clean up the dishes while Bella followed Jeb out and down to midships to his sewing room, which was actually the crew's shared sleeping quarters. Lanterns hung from hooks next to hammocks that hung from the ceiling in a row, and the open space had chairs and a table strewn with empty mugs and cards from some unfinished game. The smell of rum and unwashed men lingered. Jeb pushed everything to the side and grabbed a basket of thread, scissors, and needles.

"I won't measure ye the way I do a man." He squirmed as if he were embarrassed at the thought. "Here, use fis string to figure out yer size."

Bella didn't know what Jeb meant, so he demonstrated by putting the string around his waist, and then up and down the length of his arms and legs. She mimicked what he had done, and Jeb pulled out a quill and ink to write down numbers on a piece of rumpled paper. She couldn't read his scrawling, but as long as he knew what he was doing, she supposed it didn't matter.

"Miss Beller, yer clothes will be finis'd before the end of the week. I'll be needin' the clothes yer wearin' to take um in since makin' somfin from scratch is too time consumin'."

"I'll go back to my quarters and change into a dress."

"I'll follow. Then ye won't need to come back 'ere."

"Thank you, Jeb. I really appreciate it."

"Is fere anyfin' else I can do for ye?"

"There is one thing." Bella bit her bottom lip. She'd asked before without a yes, but the idea of being at Jasper's mercy had her blood run as cold as a winter in France. "In New Orleans, I was learning how to defend myself with a sword. I'm afraid if I don't continue practicing the skill, I'll never become proficient. Could you duel with me?"

Jeb shuffled his feet. and his voice squeaked when he answered. "I don' know if tha' is a good idea."

"This is a pirate ship, after all, and everyone knows that pirates attack other vessels. Shouldn't I be able to help defend the ship?"

"Then ye should ask the cap'n."

Bella sighed heavily. She expected that answer. "Surely the captain is too busy. I don't want to be a burden now. Or later, if something happens and the ship is in trouble."

"I'll pro'ect ye 'til my dyin' day, miss," Jeb said, his dirty cheeks flushing slightly. "But tell ye wha', if ye insist on practice training, I'll work with ye."

Relief tumbled over her, and she beamed at him. "You do me a great service."

"But I won' until yer clothes 're done. We'll be a' sea fer a while. We got time for swordplay." He nodded his head toward the stairs leading to the gallery.

"I'll ask Will to fence with ye, too."

"Oh thank you!" The thought of Quinn made her pause. It should have been him training her and this conversation was a painful reminder. She added, "I don't want to be a burden."

"Jus' lookin' at ye is help." He grinned. "Yur beau'iful, and though we can't have ye, we can dream about ye."

Bella cringed. How was she going to get anyone on her side if they thought of her like that? If she couldn't quite trust them or could barely tolerate them? She wrenched her mind back under control. *Focus on Jeb's positive traits, Bella. There are precious few people here who care if you are safe.*

Jeb led her back to the captain's cabin, and she slipped inside to change. She pulled on a pale green dress, then reemerged to find him waiting. When she handed the shirt and trousers to him, Jeb avoided eye contact.

"Thank you, Jeb," she began. "Is there time for you to show me how to reach the upper deck?"

As if by magic, Sven appeared. "I can do that. Jeb, you may attend your other duties."

Jeb trotted off, but while Sven led her in silence through the narrow passages, she wasn't memorizing her way around the ship. Instead, curiosity had the upper hand. How had Sven known she and Jeb were finished with the measurements and had returned to her quarters? More importantly, would he side with Jasper if the choice was between her honor and the captain's wishes?

"Where were you before now?" she finally asked.

"I didn't go anywhere," Sven said over his shoulder. "I've been watching you this whole time." He stopped and turned. Bella almost ran into him. "I wanted Jeb to think he was alone with you to test his trustworthiness. I wouldn't have allowed him to touch you in any way per Captain Falcon's orders, but you won Jeb over."

She blushed at the thought of having pirates loyal to her. "It seems the men respect you enough to obey."

"Yes, but it is a long journey, and you are the only woman on this ship."

Bella's skin crawled at the implications of Sven's words. Refusing to appear a victim, she straightened her spine and shoulders and followed Sven over the stinking bilge and up ladders. She caught up with him and focused on trying to memorize all the corridors and stairs they took without seeming to map a route of escape.

"Sven? Where did you live before joining this crew?" Bella asked. "You obviously weren't raised on a pirate's ship."

"Does it show?" He smirked. "I joined the crew a few years before we arrived in Port New Orleans. The *Black Fear* raided my ship and killed everyone but me. We had been privateers for King George and hadn't stooped to the level of becoming actual pirates, but I'm a healer. Captain Starr spared my life."

Bella blinked in surprise. "Jasper wasn't the original captain of this ship?"

"No, but it is best not to bring Starr up to anyone. He's deceased, and that is all you need to know."

The unspoken order not to ask made Bella suspect that whatever had happened to Starr, his death wasn't from natural causes.

"Well," she said, accepting the change of subject, "I imagine the Black Fear needs a surgeon."

"Yes." Sven sounded thoughtful. "I'm also the one who told him about Ageless Isle."

The hairs on Bella's neck prickled because from her experience, people with ties to anything magical, weren't as they appeared.

"And how did you know about the supposed magical place?"

"My previous ship was bound there, so I know the way."

They reached the upper deck, and the air blew away some of the stench. The brisk wind played with strands of hair that had escaped her ribbon.

Sven leaned in close and whispered, "I'm valuable to Captain Falcon, which means he'll keep me alive. It would be beneficial for you to find something to make you vital too."

Was that a hint about how easily her life could end if Jasper wanted her gone? She swallowed.

"Have you ever refused to do what Jasper asked?"

"While, I don't refuse him, I find ways to avoid certain commands," Sven quietly replied. "As a healer, I vowed to do no harm, so I've never had to kill anyone, though he uses my knowledge of medicinal herbs to sway people—enemies or not—when necessary." He took a furtive glance around. "But I will protect your virtue as long as I can without raising the captain's suspicions."

A shiver ran down her arms. "Why are you helping me?"

"I had a daughter like you once." Although Sven's gaze drifted to the horizon, the older man's eyes glistened. "She and my wife died on a ship from Norway, and nothing in my knowledge of remedies could prevent their deaths. If my daughter had lived and I had died in her place, I would hope that someone would have protected her too."

Bella put a hand on his arm. "Your secret is safe with me."

"Thank you." Sven pressed his palms together, and his somber expression lightened. "The crew have some wild stories about me. They think I have magic because I'm the fae king."

Sven? A fae king? Bella chuckled. "And what makes them think that?"

He shrugged. "Perhaps my knowledge of herbs?"

"Does that bother you?"

"No, I don't mind. It keeps them on their best behavior around me, which is useful since I'm not a skilled fighter."

Bella sighed. "I understand that too well, though I have had some training and hope to convince the men to help me hone my skills."

Sven shook his head. "These men are every bit as vile as you can imagine, and Captain Falcon is—"

"Is what?"

Bellas startled and spun to find Jasper at her side. A quiet gasp escaped her lips and then panic tightened her throat. Had Jasper heard her discussion with Sven? She looked toward the ocean rather than directly at Jasper, and her voice quivered slightly when she managed, "Sven was telling me that you would know how I could be helpful during this journey."

Jasper flashed a tight smile. Bella couldn't help noticing how white his teeth were—a stark contrast from Jeb's blackened gap-toothed grin.

"Sven is correct. I know what needs to be done aboard and could find something to help you pass time, but as I said before, you won't need to work aboard my vessel." Instead of reprimanding them he motioned to Bella and the line between his brows disappeared. "I want to show you something. Follow me."

Bella and Sven stepped behind Jasper, and when they reached the quarter deck, the sailors had clustered at the rail.

Sven muttered, "Too soon."

Before she could ask Sven what he meant, Jasper held a tubular monocle to her eye. "Look over there."

Bella peered in the direction Jasper had indicated. She nearly dropped it in disbelief.

Diving in and out of the water were... mermaids.

She shot a look at Jasper, whose expression was hard to read, and raised the spyglass again. After her experiences at the de la Rose plantation, she shouldn't doubt the existence of fanciful beings, but the mermaid sighting left her in awe.

A vision flashed across the view before her. A library's ceiling mural where mermaids dove in and out of the painting.

She shook her head and looked again. No, she couldn't be imagining them. They weren't what she had pictured from stories. Their hair matched their tails in hues of iridescent blue, green, purple, red, yellow, pink, brown, black, white, and orange. The shiny, gray-skinned dolphins that accompanied them seemed dull in comparison.

"We shouldn't get too close to them and take any chances," Sven cautioned.

Jasper huffed. "You're probably right. We can't afford to lose any of the men to sea witches."

"They're beautiful," Bella breathed, though she said nothing about the question of mermen.

As if the thought summoned them, mermen swooshed out of the water, but at their side. How appropriate that while the mermaids frolicked with dolphins, the mermen swam with sharks.

"Until I saw them with my own eyes, I honestly thought..." Jasper's voice hitched. "Well, I thought mermaids were mythical, even if Sven told me merfolk live on Ageless Isle. He's never been there, so how would he know?"

"You might be surprised of what I know," Sven said.

"This is proof that the fantastical things I've recently experienced weren't parts of a dream." Bella's stomach fluttered at seeing her storybooks come to life. "I only ever read about hidden wonders before now."

"Sven, I'm beginning to believe that Ageless Island will really hold all the treasures you bragged that it would." Jasper's sparkling blue eyes and raised eyebrows reminded Bella of a child opening presents on Christmas Day. He offered the sincerest smile she had seen yet.

"You won't be disappointed you kept me on your ship," Sven said.

"When we get to Ageless Isle, we'll be able to get enough treasure to live comfortably for a long time." Jasper rubbed his hook.

She shouldn't jab at the captain—her arguments with Gerard should have taught her as much, and she was more at this man's mercy than she had ever been at Gerard's—but the words spilled out, nonetheless. "You're greedy. There is more to life than gaining riches."

Sven's lips pursed.

Jasper clenched his right fist. "You know nothing of me." He then sucked in a huge breath. "But aye, treasure is my heart's desire—except..." His head turned to the ocean and then back to Bella. "I may have room in it for someone else."

Her jaw tightened. "You can't win my heart, and I'm not meant for the sea."

Jasper looked her up and down. "I think you fit in nicely, but I'm not going to lie. I have confidence I will be able to change your mind. Then perhaps I'll retire my pirate ways after we take what we can from the island." He gazed off into the horizon. "Maybe we could settle down and start a family on a plantation in New Orleans."

"Sir, would you ever be able to settle on land?" Sven asked.

"Maybe if I had the right motivation."

Bella cringed. Not only could a pirate's promises not be trusted, but her heart belonged to Quinn. She had to get away from Jasper.

"Sven, do you think you could take me to Jeb? I haven't found my way around this ship yet. I want to see if he needs any help with my new outfit."

He nodded. "If the captain doesn't need me."

"Go ahead, Sven, and give her a ship's tour." Jasper met Bella's eyes. "Someday I believe you'll be relaxed enough around me to stay, but I won't force you."

He's wrong. I will never be comfortable around him and I don't want to be here.

While she followed Sven through the bowels of the ship, Jasper's comment about leaving the pirate life to start a family ran through her head. Only true love would make a marriage last.

She would rather be a poor old maid than live trapped in a loveless marriage, and even if she didn't care for Quinn, the pirate captain would never love anything but his treasures.

Chapter 14

Jasper

The white-gold moon hung in the blackened sky, and stars dotted the vast space like twinkling diamonds. A warm breeze brushed Jasper's skin. It was disappointing that no more mermaids broke the sea's surface. The *Black Fear* had reached an uncharted world when it had left the Mississippi River and entered the sea overnight, but the mermaid sighting confirmed they were no longer in an ocean Jasper knew.

Had he truly recognized a grown-up version of the fire-haired mermaid from his boyhood dreams through the spyglass? The comfort in her gentle touch, the way her kindness—real or imagined—eased the pain after his mother's vicious beatings. Pain from the past was buried deep, and no amount of fighting had erased it completely. But the day he'd run away from home was also the day he had encountered the mermaid's tenderness.

He scanned the water for any sign of her.

Where is she?

The gentle breath of wind played with his hair. Jasper shoved his hair back into its tail, and his jaw tensed.

Brooding over a mermaid?

Bah! Ridiculous.

It was better to turn his thoughts to Ageless Isle's treasures. Doubt flickered for a moment. What if Sven had promised falsely, only to escape death? Still, he had foretold of merfolk and magic.

And Jasper's mind was back on that red-haired mermaid. Impossible. Mermaids had to stay in the water, though, so any chance at having her for his own was preposterous. Although, hadn't she grown legs when she helped him as a boy? The memory chided him for his brutal behavior, so he shook off the recollection.

"Mermaids," he growled. "Sea witches, more like."

He forced himself to remember Bella in that sea-green dress that made her creamy complexion glow, but calling up Bella's image brought back her bold comments about never being his. Fury rose to push other feelings aside. He focused on that instead.

Bella was a real, flesh-and-blood woman who could wash the mermaid from his mind.

Jasper spun on his heel and climbed down the stairs from the quarterdeck. He stormed past the crew, who were snoring loudly in hammocks or gambling at their filthy table, and ignored any pointed looks. In a matter of moments, he was outside his own cabin. *His*. It would never be Bella's room no matter how long she stayed on his ship.

His conscience prickled, but he shoved that response away.

He grunted. After all, he'd allowed her to think she was safe to lure her into trusting him. Either she'd come over to his side tonight or he'd toss her off the ship. There was no room on the *Black Fear* for a useless passenger.

He pounded on the door twice. "Knock, knock, Bella."

She opened the door, and Jasper pushed past her into the cabin. He pulled off his cravat and struggled out of his crimson damask waistcoat, then tossed them onto his chair. If his tattooed chest showed through the loosened shirt collar, all the better.

Bella gawked briefly, and then her cheeks colored. She looked away. "What do you want?"

Not the answer he'd been hoping for, and his conscience demanded that he leave.

No, he snarled inwardly.

"I came to get my bedclothes." He crossed to the armoire but couldn't hold the latch with only one hand. After several tries, the mechanism remained locked in place. He pounded the hook against the wood.

"Blast these doors. The sea air warps them."

"Here," came a soft voice at his side. "Let me help you."

Bella lifted the latch.

"I didn't need help until Aerowyn and her mangy dog boarded my ship," he growled.

"I'm sure Gerard wasn't mangy," Bella said with a gentle smile that made the red-haired mermaid vanish from his mind, "but I guess he didn't win you over after he bit off your hand."

Jasper reached his good hand to open the wardrobe, and their hands slightly brushed. He didn't pull away and when she didn't either, he released the door and pulled her against his chest. Bella tugged backward, but he held her in place.

Jasper raised his hook to brush a lock of hair from her cheek, and all color drained from her face. The fear and anger made him feel powerful.

"You want me, Bella," he rasped. "Stop resisting."

Bella writhed.

"Unhand me!"

With one tremendous shove, Bella wiggled free. Jasper reached for her, but his metal appendage pulled him back. It anchored his arm down, dragging him away from Bella. The more he resisted, the harder the hook jerked him toward the exit. His temples throbbed as he strained against the thing.

Out of the corner of his eye, he saw the fear on Bella's face shift as her green eyes scrutinized him.

His hook grew heavier, and his muscles burned from fighting it. Sweat dripped from his hairline. Jasper lost control of his legs and planted face-first onto the floor. He labored to pull himself up, but the hook yanked him back onto his knees.

"Are you drunk?" Bella asked.

"No, this hook has a mind of its own," he panted. "I can't get up."

"It's hexed!"

Jasper seethed. His blood boiled, and he put all his strength into getting back onto his feet.

"Bah! That witch..."

Bella covered her mouth which muted a giggle.

"Are you laughing at me wench?"

"I'm trying not to." She tightened her mouth into a line. "This situation is not amusing at all, but sometimes stress brings out inappropriate reactions from me."

"Help me up!"

Her laughter subsided. "I'll help you if you promise to keep your hand and hook to yourself. I told you I will never be your mistress, and I meant it."

That was the crux of the matter, wasn't it? What had that witch said? The hook would protect Bella, or something like that? He drew a deep breath and forced a confession: "Aerowyn must have cursed this blasted silver to stop me. If she did, I won't be able to touch you against your will."

At the admission, the magnetic pull loosened its grasp, and Jasper staggered to his feet, but kept a safe distance between him and Bella.

"Don't tell anyone what happened here." Jasper squared his shoulders. Repressed emotion made his voice harsh, even in his own ears. "The enchantress may have protected you from my advances, but she can't stop me from throwing you off this ship, or worse. If I find you are more of a burden than a benefit, I will have zero regret in feeding you to the sharks onboard or overboard. Do I make myself clear?"

Bella's face paled, and she clutched her arms tightly across her chest. "Yes, I understand you perfectly."

The fear dripping off of her was like a tonic, and his pulse returned to normal. Brutality was a last resort, but it worked. Bella wouldn't laugh at him again. Jasper turned and left the room slamming the door, scowling when the lock clicked in place behind him.

To cool his irritation and temperature, he stomped to the stern of the upper deck for fresh air. If Bella wouldn't give into his charms, he would tire of the game and send her to Davy Jone's Locker with zero regrets.

"Jasper."

He spun around, but Bella had locked herself in the cabin. Then who—

"Jasper," sang the woman's voice again.

None of the men on deck reacted, but something drew Jasper to the side of the ship. The red of her hair muted by the moonlight, the mermaid of his memories floated alongside the bow. He swiveled to see if anyone else noticed how close she was, but the crew remained oblivious.

When he looked back, the beauty was still there.

"How—" He lowered his voice. "How do you know my name?"

"Don't you remember me?" she asked as quietly as he had, "When you were a boy, I dried your tears."

Jasper blinked rapidly. "I thought that was a dream."

"No, I'm real. I've been following you closely after our encounter. Since you joined the *Black Fear* immediately, it was easy."

Jasper glanced over his shoulder nervously, but the men continued their work as if neither of them were there.

"Don't worry."

Her wide eyes mesmerized him. Were they still green? Was that why he was entranced by Bella's?

The mermaid continued, "I've cast a spell to mute our conversation. No others can hear it. I'm invisible to everyone but you."

"What's your name?" he asked.

"I'm Cerise, but I told you that years ago when we were seven."

The memories rushed back after Cerise triggered them. This pretty sea maiden had healed the bruises from one of his beatings.

"Yes, now I remember." Jasper's heart thumped in his chest. *Cerise is real.* "I had forgotten. I didn't mean to. I shouldn't... But why did you wait to talk to me after all these years?"

"I didn't want to interfere. But oh, Jasper, I'm disappointed in you. And after I showed you kindness and magic."

"What do you mean?" he whispered, but he knew. The truth was in the hook on his hand and locked in his cabin.

"You shouldn't have kidnapped that girl." With that, the mermaid leaped, and her tail disappeared into the ocean.

"Cerise," he called out, not caring who heard him.

She didn't resurface.

Jasper waited, but Cerise was gone.

Her words pierced him. Regret had never played a large part in his mind, but suddenly he had many.

Chapter 15

Bellarose

T he door slammed. Bella quickly locked it and somehow shoved the trunk to block it, even though her whole body shook from the effort. If Jasper really wanted in, a locked door and wooden trunk wouldn't stop him. She fell into a nearby chair before her wobbly legs collapsed and focused on breathing in and out. Any thoughts of a relaxing evening had vanished when he pounded on the door. After what felt like ages, her racing heart gradually slowed.

Prior to when Jasper pulled her against his chest, he had been well-behaved, and she had foolishly believed that the man would respect her virtue.

Bella palmed her forehead. What was she thinking when she laughed at him? He was dangerous. Her nerves had finally made her insane, for no matter how much of a gentleman Jasper pretended to be, he was a foul man determined to have his prey.

A shiver ran down Bella's spine. Gerard would have found a way to turn her laughter into a compliment. Resentment crept in. Yes, Aerowyn had hexed Jasper's hook, but why hadn't the enchantress rescued Bella from the ship instead? Even a cursed metal appendage couldn't stop a ship full of pirates from coming after her.

What if I escape on that lifeboat Sven showed me?

Fright replaced common sense, and she pushed the trunk back, turned the key in the lock and sneaked down the passageway. Bella found her way onto the main deck and managed to reach the lifeboat without being seen. Thick ropes twisted around wood, and though she tried to figure out how to lower it into the ocean, it didn't drop an inch.

A touch on her shoulder made Bella yelp.

"What are you doing?" Sven whispered.

"I'm escaping before Jasper kills me."

Sven patted her shoulder. "I won't let him do that. Besides you can't survive long on the ocean without food and water, and the *Black Fear* will be able to catch you."

"You're right." Bella slumped in defeat, and tears ran down her face. "What was I thinking?"

"Why don't you let me take you back to your room?" Sven wrapped his arm around her shoulder. "I always think clearer after a good night's sleep."

The first mate led her to the cabin and instructed her to lock the door. Bella obeyed and climbed into bed. The ship swayed gently, and waves slapped its sides. Gradually Bella drifted into dreams where Quinn was the one who chopped off Jasper's hand, and then he saved her from the pirates.

She woke disturbed, yet oddly refreshed. The chances of seeing Quinn again were small. If he received her letter, he chose to stay in Louisiana. If he hadn't... Well, she had no way of knowing what had happened, and the truth was she really couldn't escape on her own. Last night's attempt was foolish, but insightful. Sven may be an ally she could trust. Renewed determination and proper sleep provided the encouragement Bella needed.

Though her dreams had been both bloody and exhilarating, Bella put them aside and dug through the trunk. A simple, light-blue dress caught her eye, so she donned it, splashed water from the basin on her face, and tied her hair back into a ribbon.

Feet stomped overhead and boisterous calls cut through her peaceful morning. Sudden fear that Jasper would reappear with expectations rushed Bella through her routine. She needed out of that cabin. Besides fresh sea air would clear her head.

She shoved the trunk back into its place and flung the door open. As she made her way up the stairs, Sven appeared as if from a mist.

"Good day, Miss Bella. Did you sleep better last night?"

Thankful that he didn't bring up her futile attempt to escape, she began, "No. Yes, but..." She couldn't bring herself to tell him of Jasper's behavior and, the reason she had tried to flee but thought better of it. "Never mind. How is it you're always nearby? Did Jasper kick you out of your room?"

"I did have to find different accommodations to give the captain his privacy. His sour mood was unbearable." Sven studied her, then whispered, "That's why I was able to stop your escape. I hope the captain didn't try anything. Was that why you were so upset?"

Her gaze shifted from him to her toes. "My virtue is still intact, but—I think it's because of that hook."

"What do you mean?"

"I know he told everyone the enchantress gave it to him. Well, I think she hexed it because it prevented him from touching me."

Sven's forehead furrowed. He fingered the pendant hanging on the simple hemp string around his neck. "Hexed, huh?"

She nodded.

The two reached the upper deck, and Bella spotted mermaids off in the distance again." Before she could point them out, Sven gently pulled Bella to the port railing. He kept his tone down, "Please be careful, Bellarose. Even with a cursed hook, he's dangerous."

She shuddered. "I know."

"Based on my calculations, we'll be on Ageless Isle tomorrow, and then you no longer have to worry about Jasper."

"Won't he be just as dangerous on the island?"

"No. I need to tell you some—" He stopped abruptly and stared at the horizon. "Are those storm clouds?"

Bella cast one more glance at the mermaids, then looked at the sky. Flattened, gray clouds were rising out of the ocean. They hid the sun and raced toward the ship.

"Those don't seem like normal clouds," Bella said as a foreshadowing of danger made her hands shake.

Sven pinched his lips, then nodded. "We're going to end up in the midst of a squall."

As he spoke the words, the clouds rushed over the ship, and torrential rain drenched them.

A pirate yelled, "Hoist the sails!"

The wind rocked the *Black Fear* back and forth wildly. Bella almost fell overboard, but Sven caught her by the arm.

"That was too sudden," he shouted over the storm. "Get back to your room, Miss Bella! Now!"

She scrambled to obey, the fear of being tossed into the sea growing every moment. If she had escaped in the small life boat last night, it would have been torn apart in this storm. The thought was as chilling as the rain.

Bella slipped on the wet deck. As she made her way aft, she fell several times. Waves washed over her, and she held onto the rail for dear life. She bit back a scream.

This wasn't how she had wanted to escape Jasper.

She wanted to live.

And one thing she found herself wishing was she would someday have the chance to tell Quinn how she really felt about him.

Chapter 16

Callista

Once Callista had played with dolphins. Once, she had been surrounded by her magnificent family, and she had been the most beautiful of them all. Once she had been best friends with the fae king's daughter, Isla.

That was before the king had cursed her.

Before she had become an outcast.

Now she could only spy on her former family from a distance.

She was isolated. No longer gorgeous. Rejected. Disgusting.

She grasped the necklace around her neck. The king thought bestowing upon her extra magical abilities with her own shell-shaped pendant would make up for her loss?

He is a fool.

As if in agreement, clouds gathered above.

She clenched her fists. *Let it rain.*

The sound of laughter caught her supernatural hearing and drew her toward her family as they frolicked in the waves. Her jaw tightened and she sank down into the depths but kept an eye on them. Spying was her communion with them now.

Do they even care that I am gone?

A shadow drifted overhead.

Callista squinted at the hull of a ship, then swam closer. Men this close to Ageless Isle? Pirates? Perhaps, but... something about that shorter rotund man on the upper deck seemed familiar. Ignoring the pretty young woman at his side, Callista focused on the old pirate.

Her blood pounded at the sight of the sparkling diamond in the center of his tear-shaped pendant.

Only one fae had an adornment like that—

King Peter.

The fae who ruined her life.

Callista's mouth turned upward while her wretched mood soared. This was her opportunity to make Peter's life as miserable as hers and maybe even foil his plans for the pirate ship, whatever they were.

The desire for revenge swallowed all thoughts of her losses. Her loneliness and the constant thought of how her beautiful, iridescent cerulean fin was replaced with a chartreuse, sea snake's one vanished. She slither-swam underneath the ship, almost grateful that her slimy ugly tail made it easier to hide. Swimming rapidly in circles underneath the vessel, she lifted the shell pendant to use the consolation prize King Peter had foolishly given her.

The ocean churned. The violent winds of a tumultuous typhoon forced the clouds across the sky. Chaotic, frothing, white-caps raced toward the ship with a deafening roar, threatening to swallow everything in its path.

Callista cackled. She would show him.

He couldn't ruin her life and get away with it.

Chapter 17

Bellarose

T he deck vibrated beneath Bella's feet as if the planks were ready to splinter. The rain blurred her vision, but Sven took her by the arm and led her down the ladder to the captain's quarters. She settled down to ride out the tempest.

The ship tilted and jostled. Thankful she never got sea sick, Bella shivered as she changed out of her wet clothes and slipped into a brown frock from the trunk. While she draped her wet dress over a chair to dry, memories of her last trip at sea blasted through her. *Mère, Père... Was that what I called them*? The scarred-over wound in her heart broke open like the cloud's violent downpour. Hot tears rolled down her already wet face but just as another wave of sorrow smacked her, the ship jerked ferociously.

Bella grabbed the bedpost. The captain's commands broke through the storm's noise and her sorrow. She wasn't familiar with the nautical terms Jasper shouted, but the urgency in his voice switched off her despondency. The situation was more dire than she had thought. Bella held on to the furniture as everything that was unsecured tipped, then fell onto the floor.

Men's desperate curses pierced through the walls, wind, and waves. Cracks appeared in the floor, and Bella shot to her feet, still clinging to the bed. The polished walls' paneling separated. The *Black Fear* floundered, and the floor tilted sideways flinging Bella into the captain's desk. She cried out.

Boards split, and water poured inside.

She had two choices: become trapped underneath a sinking ship to drown or risk the violent ocean.

The waves seemed a safer risk, so she swayed to her feet, falling multiple times, and made her way to the upper deck only in time to see the masts cracked. Horrified, she watched them lean into the ocean.

The weight of the partially furled sails forced the *Black Fear* to dip into the churning storm. Men cursed and shrieked, holding on for dear life to whatever they could reach. Everyone, including the mighty Captain Falcon, was hurled into the chaotic water.

Alone on the fractured deck, out-of-breath, with panic tightening her throat, Bella stumbled toward the broken mast and grabbed a plank. Slivers punctured her hands, and her muscles burned from the effort to walk straight without falling.

In vain, she screamed for help. No one was left. Then, like everyone else, her battered body was pitched into the sea.

Chapter 18

Callista

Callista surfaced to watch the ship splinter apart. It didn't take long for the craft to sink, forcing all souls into the raging sea. She smirked. It wasn't complete vindication for what King Peter had done to her, but as the ship vanished, a smug satisfaction swelled.

She scanned the waves. If only everyone would drown, including Peter.

But the powerful fae king could easily escape the ocean's clutches, and even if Peter couldn't break free, there was the inconvenient fact that he was immortal. Eventually, he would float onto the shore of his island. At the very least, he had been rendered powerless for a little while.

Her lips curved upward.

Spotting the king on that pirate ship had been true luck.

All she needed now was the opportunity to steal Peter's power and undo his curse.

Perhaps her chance was closer than she had thought.

Chapter 19

Sven

The storm had attacked as if controlled by a magical being. Everyone had been tossed into the sea, and with them all struggling to stay afloat, no one paid attention to Sven.

He murmured a phrase and waved one hand. The tumultuous waves calmed. Although, he could have stopped the storm completely, he wasn't ready to reveal himself as the immortal fae king. Not yet.

And that wasn't Sven's priority. He needed to find Bella, so he swam effortlessly in the now peaceful ocean searching for her. A booming voice turned him around to see a small lifeboat heading in his direction.

Jasper barked out orders, and the rescued pirates rowed up faster.

"Sven, you're alive!" A thin smile of relief stretched over Jasper's face. "Come aboard."

While King Peter was immortal and strong, Sven, he reminded himself, was not. He held out a hand and allowed the captain to help him into the boat. The captain gritted his teeth. Evidently, having only one hand, made it harder to pull Sven up.

"Oof, Sven! You need to lay off the grog," Jasper huffed. His smirk vanished as he finished, "Welcome on board the *Mighty Jasper*, which is the only thing left of the *Black Fear*."

"You know I don't partake in such refreshments, captain." Sven forced a grimace. "Though, I do have trouble turning down extra helpings at dinner time."

Jeb patted Sven on the back hard. "Good to see ye, Sven."

Sven surveyed the glassy ocean for Bella, who been wearing a muted blue dress. He frowned. That material would have blended in with the water.

Without looking away from the waves, he said, "You, too, Jeb. Has anyone seen Bella?"

"No, but Cap'n has been lookin'."

Jasper gave Sven a crooked grin. "I believe the beautiful Miss Bonnay may have sunk to the bottom of the ocean."

Sven studied the captain using his fae abilities. Jasper certainly had conflicted thoughts over the prospect of Bellarose's demise. He felt it served Bella right for rejecting him, but Sven also detected remorse. Something—or someone—had rebuked his behavior toward Miss Bonnay and the captain didn't want to accept that emotion yet.

Interesting.

Sven frowned. "If she was able to hang on to a floating piece of wood, she may still be alive."

He needed her to be alive.

"By all means, Sven, go ahead. You're fit-as-a-fiddle and will easily find the contemptuous Bellarose." Jasper pointed his hook toward the vastness beyond, and the sarcasm rolled off his tongue. "I. for one. am sorry I brought her on our ship in the first place. She was obviously bad luck and didn't benefit me at all. Good riddance."

"I made Bella go inside your cabin during the storm. She could be trapped in the wreckage at the bottom of the sea."

"Then it's too late." Jasper shrugged. "I don't think she's daft enough to stay inside a sinking vessel, but if she drowned, she drowned." He turned away, but Sven heard him mutter, "No regrets and never look back."

Jasper's inner monologue sent a different message. The light and darkness inside him were fighting for control. Sven went back to scanning the waves on which sailors bobbed up and down like corks in a barrel.

Will and Jeb exchanged uneasy glances, but they rowed to rescue their crewmates. Sven managed to enlarge the small craft without anyone noticing each time a man was lifted into it.

He tapped his fingers on the bow. He'd only been on the *Black Fear* to protect Bella, though his daughter didn't understand why he had to guard the girl. It took two years of living with despicable pirates to set the stage for his plan and to gain their trust.

"Father," she'd said, "it's highly unusual for a fae king to protect a mortal."

Maybe he should've told Aerowyn that Bellarose's fate was tied into the destiny of all fairy tales. It was imperative she had a happily-ever-after to end the mess his inconsolable grief had created in the first place.

Sven's lips went into a line. Where was Bella, and why did Jasper, one of the vilest men he'd had the displeasure of knowing, survive? Yes, Jasper's was one of many stories that could be redeemed with proper magical direction, but the fae king wasn't hopeful about that despite the man's regrets. Even if the captain was rethinking his choices, Sven cared less about Jasper's inner turmoil than he did for Bella's safety.

Minutes passed. This was taking too long. Sven was about to cast off his disguise to search for the girl when a mermaid with flame-colored hair surfaced, holding Bella's unconscious head above the water.

"Hurry," the mermaid demanded. "Help me get this girl into your boat."

Jasper's eyes widened with obvious recognition, and Sven frowned. How did a pirate know this mermaid?

"There's no time to waste," the mermaid continued. "Pull me up. She's not breathing, and I can help her."

Without hesitation and with only one arm, Jasper roughly hefted her into the craft as well.

As soon as the mermaid was out of the water, her fins transformed into legs. She moved quickly to resuscitate Bella. Though her long, red hair covered most of her naked form, the pirates ogled her anyway. Jasper took off his oversized shirt and draped it over the now-human mermaid who pushed on Bella's chest and breathed into her mouth. Once, twice, three times. Then Bella rolled to her side, vomited up sea water, and coughed.

The mermaid gently pushed a lock of water-darkened hair from Bella's face. "How are you feeling miss?"

"Sore." Bella's words came out raspy. "Who, who are you?"

"I'm Cerise."

"Cerise saved you from the sunken ship and was able to get you to breathe again," Jasper interjected too loudly.

"What happened?" Bella winced as she sat up.

"The storm forced us all into the ocean, but this mermaid helped you."

"Than—" A coughing fit stopped Bella's words, then she croaked out, "Thank you."

"I knew that sea witch, Callista was planning something." Cerise put her arms into Jasper's shirtsleeves, straightened the shirt around her knees, and buttoned it up. "She's always lurking around waiting for an opportunity to create havoc and mayhem."

Sven threw a glance over his shoulder. Yes, the devastation resembled one of Callista's tantrums. The more he thought about it, the more certain he was she was to blame for the sudden typhoon. He rubbed the back of his neck and surveyed the damage.

Bella scrunched her nose at the men and carefully maneuvered her body to be a barrier between the pirates and the mermaid. There wasn't a lot of room on the boat, but Bella's protectiveness seemed to give the men a temporary conscience. They averted their gazes and cleared their throats.

"I need to go back to my people." Cerise handed Jasper his shirt, then dove into the ocean. Her head and torso dunked below the surface as her iridescent red fin sprung up briefly before disappearing from view.

"Cerise," Jasper boomed, "wait!"

Her head popped above the water and her lips curved upwards bashfully.

"Before you go," Jasper said, "we will be in your debt for saving Bella's life. If anyone ever gives you trouble, tell them that Captain Jasper Falcon is your friend and champion. I will fight for you."

She blushed. "It is a kind offer, Captain. Thank you."

With a flick of her tail, she swam away.

Sven frowned. The young mermaid seemed flattered by Jasper's attention, but the man couldn't fight her enemies, if she had any. Enemies of mermaids would all be magic users. And Sven doubted that he really cared if Cerise saved Bella's life.

"Where are we anyway?" Bella's voice sounded strained.

"I don't have my navigation tools," Sven said, "but it doesn't seem the storm took us too far off our course."

The truth was that he would need magic to get the lifeboat to Ageless Isle. They were actually far off course, and though he had wanted to wait until they were on the island to show his true identity, Callista had changed those plans.

After they completely searched the area around the sunken *Black Fear* and rescued as many men as they could, they summed up their losses. Only eleven of his men survived and one hundred were gone. When Jeb's eyes welled up with tears, Jasper frowned.

"Those who perished in the storm knew the risk," Jasper said. "Sailors are willing to face the dangers for a free life on sea." He lifted his hook. "Cheer up! Now you will have even more treasure to keep for yourself from Ageless Isle."

Jeb gave a weak smile that didn't reach his eyes. "Aye aye, Cap'n."

Did Jasper truly mean what he said? Sven fought back a grimace while he read Jasper's thoughts. The captain's emotions weren't buried too deeply. It seemed after losing his wealth to Callista's destruction, the captain was putting on a brave front for the men but was also relieved there were fewer of them to share the wealth. As far as Jasper could tell, his first problem was that with fewer men, they couldn't man a ship large enough to carry all the treasure he hoped to find on the island. Jasper's bigger problem was that as far as he knew, there were no ships to be had in the middle of the Caribbean Sea.

Sven smirked as he settled back onto the wooden plank seat. Luckily for everyone in this magically expanded lifeboat, that supposedly bigger problem was within his power to fix.

Chapter 20

Jasper

Jasper surveyed the surrounding water with despondency. All he had left from the wreckage was his hidden knife strapped around his left leg. They were in the middle of the ocean without food or water, and a vivid image of sharks swimming with mermen made Jasper cringe inwardly. He'd faked that jovial smile to rally his men, but the chances they'd find land before they died of dehydration were next to zero. He'd gave his surviving crew what they needed: cocky over-the-top confidence.

He ground his teeth. He should have thought to ask Cerise for help to the island, but when she blushed, he felt invincible. *Idiot.* She was the girl he'd always dreamed of having. The one who surpassed any other woman, including Bella. Jasper's perfect girl existed, and despite the realization that all his possessions were now at the bottom of the sea, he couldn't get Cerise out of his mind.

He shook off thoughts of the stunning red-head. Their current predicament was going to become dire and he needed a plan.

Jeb interrupted Jasper's ponderings, "Cap'n? Whut we goin' do abou' the shark?"

Jasper yanked his mind back to the present, in time to see a gray dorsal fin bumping the lifeboat. Though terror was etched on the men's faces and Bella's hands shook, Sven remained calm, which wasn't like the man, but Jasper didn't think too much of it with the imminent danger taking all his concentration.

"Do you all want to live?" Sven called out.

Several mumbled yes in shaky voices, and others merely managed a nod.

"Then I need you to stay calm and seated. I am going to reveal my true identity."

Sven mumbled in a language Jasper didn't recognize—and he had been to a lot of ports. The first mate seemed to shimmer, like Aerowyn had back in New Orleans, then he transformed into a tall, well-built, white-haired young man. He spoke more gibberish, and the shark swam away.

Jasper gulped. The crew gaped speechless.

"Who are you?" Bella rasped out.

"I'm King Peter. Aerowyn the enchantress is my daughter."

Bella gasped.

"We live on Ageless Isle. I was going to reveal my identity on the island, but Callista's storm changed that. Also, the shark wouldn't have left us alone if I hadn't become my true self and ordered it to leave."

"Well, *Peter*," Jasper spat out. "You've been holding out on me."

"If you only knew how much, but that isn't currently important." The king repeated a phrase in a different language over and over again, then called, "Tilly!"

A speck of light flew toward them, and as it drew near, Jasper saw it was a tiny curvy woman with wings and pink hair.

"Tilly, this is the crew of the *Black Fear,* or at least what was left of it after Callista used a typhoon to destroy it. We need to go to Ageless Isle, and I need your assistance."

Tilly's sharp voice was barely audible, but Peter seemed to understand her. He replied in the unfamiliar language, and the lifeboat magically grew a mast and sail.

Tilly flew above them and shook her body all over the canvas. Glittering dust flaked over the white cloth, making it sparkle. Then the vessel shifted, straightened, and rose out of the water. Soon the craft was airborne. Jasper's stomach dropped, and his heart thumped wildly. It reminded him of the first time he climbed the tallest mast.

Tilly flew to whisper in Peter's ear. He nodded, and she zoomed away. A few men gawked after the tiny, winged woman until she disappeared from sight.

"Bloody—"

"Jeb," Peter interrupted, "we still have a lady in our presence. Please refrain from cursing."

"Oops. Sorry, Mis'er King or Sven—um—or whatever it is I should call ye."

The other pirates leaned in to hear Peter's reply.

"You may call me King Peter, King, or Your Majesty." He turned his gaze to the horizon. "Only my closest friends are allowed to call me Peter."

All the men bowed their heads reverently, but Jasper grimaced at *Peter's* pompous words. This was the man he had begun to trust and now he supposedly was the father of a cruel enchantress, even though he looked the same age as Aerowyn. No matter, Peter had ulterior motives.

The lifeboat-turned-sailing ship soared over the ocean, and a cool briny breeze wafted over Jasper. The air chilled as they glided above the billowing clouds. Stars seemed barely out of reach. It wasn't nighttime, but the glittering diamond-like things hung brightly in the sky. Jasper forced his mouth shut when his hair bristled over his body. He refused to show awe or look ridiculous as Jeb and the other men who appeared half-way between drunk and stupefied.

Bella, however, had the expression of pure ecstasy as her smile widened. "This reminds me of stories I've read about fairies and flying ships."

"Only Tilly's magical pixie dust could carry this group to the island," Peter explained.

"We're no longer flying over the Atlantic Ocean. Where are we exactly?" Jasper asked.

"We're near the second star to the right, where dreams and nightmares exist," the king said matter-of-factly.

Jasper sighed. "What does that even mean?"

"It's complicated."

Peter faced Jasper and said sternly, "The phrase 'where dreams and nightmares exist' means that while you may find a boat-load of treasure to achieve your every dream, Ageless Isle has many nightmares."

"And what about the other nonsense, 'the second star to the right?' Where exactly is that?"

Peter pointed up. "You see the brightest star in the sky? That is where my ancestors were born. We call it Cigam."

"Cigam?" Bella asked, wonder in her voice.

Peter turned to her. "Yes. Our navigation is based around that star. We will be going to an island that is located directly in line with the second star to the right of Cigam beyond the human zone." He rubbed his chin. "Before Ageless Isle, we lived in the Kingdom of Magic, which was closer to the mortals' realm."

Bella squeaked out, "I read about why you left the Kingdom of Magic in *The Scorned Fae!*" Her excitement vanished, and she swallowed hard. "The story wasn't a fictional fairy tale, was it?"

Peter crossed his arms. "All fairy tales you have read are originated in truth, but the characters don't live in your world. We live adjacent. That's why people have trouble accepting that magic and mythical creatures really exist." He uncrossed his arms and touched the pendant around his neck. "We have always kept to our own side of folklore to prevent the stories from impacting your people. Unfortunately, things have changed, and our stories are bleeding over into your lives, creating new tales not in the ancient manuscripts."

"Bah! That's utter nonsense." Jasper started to cross his arms, but his hook snagged his ruined coat. Yet another reason to be angry at lying, deceptive fae. "Why didn't your ancestors stay on Cigam? How do you even know that's where they're from?"

Peter fixed Jasper with a cold iron gaze. "We'd burn up if we lived on a star. After birth, my people were attached to a comet and hurled to Earth with the fireproof manuscripts detailing our past. Cigam is only a place of origin, never a residence for living creatures." He paused to survey the broad expanse out in front of them. Then he waved his hand, and the air warmed.

"Your Majesty," Bella began, but the king rudely interrupted her.

"The fae chose to live in a land adjacent to humans in the Kingdom of Magic, which was separated from the human realm by the dark forest. We cannot tolerate the mythical creatures who live in the human zone. I had another daughter named Isla who learned that the hard way." Peter's shoulders drooped. "After that incident, we left the Kingdom of Magic and relocated to Ageless Isle."

Bella patted Peter's arm. "I'm sorry."

Jasper's lip curled in disgust. The way she treated Peter after his deceit was sickening. Neither he nor his precious daughter could be trusted. Aerowyn took Jasper's hand, after all. And why was this king on the *Black Fear* in the first place and why in a disguise? Was he lying about riches on Ageless Isle too? The fae was leaving out important information. Wasn't that what they did?

The betrayal of Sven being a lie bothered Jasper more than he wanted to admit. He'd liked the man.

"If your ancestors came from a star," Bella asked, "is that where you all came from?"

"My ancestors did. We can marry and have children, as humans do. My wife, Wendy wasn't fae. I met her during my wild youth, and we fell in love. Wendy died of old age a long time ago." Peter's facial muscles tightened. "She didn't have to face the tragedies our people have been forced to experience."

Jasper stared at the fae king. "Wendy died of old age? Does that mean your immortal?"

Peter pursed his lips and nodded.

That explains why he looks so young.

What did this Peter have up his sleeve? Jasper might not care about the king's feelings, but he needed to know that information. If the fae were immortal, why didn't Peter help his wife live forever?

No one with Peter's powers understood true suffering like Jasper had when he was a boy and starvation was only a bit less painful than his father's fist. "What tragedy could someone with so much magic face?"

Peter remained fixated on the horizon.

"It's in the book I mentioned." Bella scowled at Jasper. "If you hadn't kidnapped me, I would have it and allow you to read it. And I think you should stop pestering King Peter about it."

Jasper couldn't lose his temper with the impertinent girl, who now had an ally against him. It was naïve for her to trust Peter, but the lines between Bella's brows finally went away and she smiled for the first time since Jasper saw her with Quinn. The crew also seemed to gravitate around Peter and hang on his words.

Though his motto was, *No regrets and no looking back*, keeping Sven alive was rapidly becoming his second regret during this trip. He needed to take back control before he lost it permanently.

Chapter 21

Bellarose

The faint smell of sulfur and ozone warmed the air. Bella gazed at the stars and puffy clouds, her mind reeling from what Peter had just told them. He was the king of the fae, and Aerowyn was his daughter. Now Bella understood what Sven had meant whenever he had promised she'd be okay. He had also said she'd be surprised by what he knew. That was an understatement.

His daughter had been Isla? From her favorite book, *The Scorned Fae*? She hadn't felt empathy for Isla when she'd read it. She'd been busy cheering for the prince and his princess to have a happy ending, which ultimately meant Isla's demise after she tried to split up the happy couple by transforming the prince into a dragon. Even after discovering the fae was Peter's daughter, she still didn't know how to feel about the selfish girl, but when the characters were fictional, Bella hadn't cared about the villain's family members' loss... Knowing Peter and Aerowyn changed things.

Grief and loss were etched all over the fae king's face. It was the same pain she saw Gerard have after he mentioned a lost love. That's when she recalled the brief downcast expression Jasper had when Cerise disappeared after saving her life. She dismissed it because she was still recovering from almost drowning.

Bella glanced at the pirate captain. He was the villain in her story, but did he have a secret agony like Gerard and Peter that turned him into this foul man? Did the anti-hero need a second chance? Did Jasper deserve that too?

If Jasper was a character in one of her books, she would have loathed him, but perhaps if she had known what turned him into a reprehensible pirate, she would wish for some kind of redemption. After all, Gerard left a horrific first impression, but once she learned what turned him into the egotistical swine, she realized he was masking his pain.

Even she used her sassy side to disguise inner turmoil and fear.

Isla probably wouldn't have ever changed her ways, but Bella now felt compassion on Peter's behalf. Jasper may never alter his behavior either, but since Aerowyn only took his hand rather than his life and hexed his hook, she must have something planned for his redemption.

Bella's chest tightened at the thought of Aerowyn. Why did the enchantress always put Bella in the thick of her projects? Did that mean Peter was part of the scheme too? She trusted him when he was Sven, but now she wondered why the king of the fae seemed so interested in protecting her. Although, until she knew, she'd not judge him too harshly.

Bella examined the men's demeanors. Peter stood with his arms crossed and Jasper glared off into the darkened sky.

Wait. The sun had been overhead when they had started their ascent. She shifted her attention away from the king and the pirate to take in this magical experience. Bella tilted her head up and immediately noticed the bright spectacle of stars.

She asked Peter, "Shouldn't it still be daytime?"

Peter nodded. "It was afternoon, but I needed the stars to navigate to Ageless Isle. I forced our vessel to move ahead slightly in time."

Jasper shouldered himself between Bella and Peter. "I thought it was pixie dust that made us fly."

"The pixie dust keeps us in the air, but I use magic to move the boat."

"Of course you do," Jasper huffed. "How silly of me to ask."

Bella bit her lower lip. The tension between the two men had been growing ever since Sven turned into Peter, and it had to be stopped.

To distract the young captain from his apparent distrust, she said brightly, "Those wisps of clouds remind me of puffy wool after it's been sheared from a sheep. Though the clouds are fluffier than wool and almost transparent, I can't think of anything else to compare them to." She chuckled. "Who would have imagined in a million years a boat could fly with dust from a pixie fae? In fact, who would know anything about such wonders?"

"Leave it to you to get excited over all of this," Jasper grumbled, then stalked away and sat beside one of his men.

Strangely, Bella felt only the slightest burst of pride that one crisis was averted. She turned back to watch King Peter. Enchantresses in her books were always dangerous. Was Peter as shifty as his daughter?

A strong breeze moved Bella's long hair into her face. Her hair-tie had been lost in the sea, so she held her loose curls to prevent them from blocking her view. Shorter strands escaped her palm and tickled her cheeks.

The air cooled. It seemed thinner somehow. Bella struggled to catch her breath. King Peter seemed to notice and said an incantation, after which the pressure left Bella's chest.

She turned to the king. "What are you saying?"

"I'm thickening the air around us to duplicate what we're accustomed to at a lower elevation with a more tepid temperature. I don't want anyone to faint or freeze."

"Oh," she said.

His words almost made sense, as if they were something she had known long, long ago and forgotten. Bella looked over the side of the boat, but couldn't see anything save clouds. A brief memory of looking out a window at clouds surfaced. People didn't fly. This was simply another of her whimsical dreams.

"Why do we have to fly so high?"

"The wind will move us more swiftly up here. If we all had pixie wings, we'd be able to fly as fast as humming birds. Tilly is probably already home in her cottage asleep."

A few seconds after Peter spoke, a sweet and spicy scent replaced the sulfur one. Bella couldn't place the fragrance, but she liked it better. The boat slowly descended, and the temperature grew even warmer. Clouds disappeared, and below them white waves brushed a shoreline. The moonlight and stars illuminated the area with a mysterious glow.

"Even if we couldn't see the land, that scent tells me Ageless Isle is below." Peter inhaled sharply. "The odors of the exotic plant life are strong. It isn't as noticeable on the ground, or they'd overwhelm us."

Jasper ambled over again. "Are those the plants you mentioned I could sell for profit?"

The fae king threw him a sharp glare. "Yes, but what ship will you load them onto?"

Jasper straightened. "I'm not going to let a pesky detail like that stop me from gaining wealth from this island. You got me here, and I expect you to lead me back."

Peter's grasp splintered the edge of the boat and his expression turned dangerous. His eyes went from brown to violet right in front of Bella. She gulped in fear. Aerowyn's eyes had done that, too.

The craft landed smoothly onto the water near the shore, and Peter said, "We have arrived."

Bella's fears vanished. It was as if she had entered a fairy tale. Peter helped her out of the boat by carrying her to the shore. His strong arms tightened against her. This sinewy Peter was nothing like her podgy friend Sven. The first mate had been a father figure, and it was hard to wrap her head around the change to a handsome fairy king.

"Bella has working legs. I'm sure she can walk as everyone else has to the shore," Jasper mumbled.

Peter bowed after he placed her effortlessly onto the shore, then said sternly, "A lady shouldn't have to get wet when a gentleman is near."

Jasper harrumphed. "I'll be the one to help her out next time if the opportunity comes again."

Was that jealousy in Jasper's voice? She understood if he mistrusted Peter, but envy made no sense. Surely, Jasper was too concerned with his treasure to care whose assistance Bella received. As before, she resolved to steer clear of him as much as possible, and her heart pinched. If Quinn were here, she would have felt safer.

The sail boat became a lifeboat once again, and the sails turned into white-winged birds and flew away. The rest of the men sloshed through the water, pulled the boat to the sand, and looked for a place to anchor it so it wouldn't float off to sea. The vessel wouldn't be adequate enough to transport the crew to their own world without magic, but it was the only form of travel they had.

"We should make camp here for the night," Peter suggested. "There are too many dangers to traverse the isle in the dark."

The hairs rose on the back of Bella's neck. "Dangers?"

"You will be safe as long as I'm here, but we don't want to run into any of them blindly."

Jasper slapped Peter on the back. "I think we can handle a few wild animals, mate."

The fae king narrowed his eyes. "Not magical ones. You have strength not supernatural powers."

Bella bit her lip again. The pirate needed to stop antagonizing the king. She didn't know what was more dangerous, Jasper or this island. Although when Peter was Sven, he said she would be protected from Jasper's evil intentions. Perhaps Peter had some more schemes up his sleeve.

The de la Rose plantation seemed a million miles away—perhaps it was—and she wanted to be there even if Quinn didn't love her.

The whole day—shipwreck, fae, pixie dust, flying ships—had been like a book, and she was convinced that adventures were highly over-rated.

Chapter 22

Jasper

J asper clenched his fists. This Peter—formerly—Sven was begging for a punch in the face.

The liar couldn't be trusted. Jasper screwed up his face, but when he noticed Peter staring at him, he smoothed it. He would play along with the witch's father and see the king's end game.

"Why don't you magic us away to our destination?" Jasper lofted an eyebrow. What was the fairy king up to and why did he really lead Jasper Ageless Isle? There had to be a way to get the fae to tell the truth. "Camping here is a waste of time when we have such a powerful fae at our disposal."

Peter glared at Jasper. "Transporting large groups of people with my magic is risky. Besides, you wanted to see this island. We'll rest tonight then walk there. It'll take a full day."

"One might think you were stalling for some reason." Jasper gave him a tight-lipped smile. "I doubt any of us will be able to sleep on the sand out in the open."

"I may not be able to transport us home, but the island's magic can use your imaginations to create comfortable accommodations," Peter replied icily. He pivoted to Bella, "Think about a bed, tent, or cabin you would enjoy using for the night."

"What do you mean?" Bella's voice rose in pitch slightly.

"Think of the best place you've ever slept," Peter said.

"I been longin' for a sof' ma'ress wif sof' blankets," Jeb piped in.

Another sailor added, "I'd like a soft wench to go with that."

"Let me remind all of you that Bella is a lady," Peter snapped. "I will not tolerate any crass or lude comments around her. You may be accustomed to saying whatever pops into your heads, but not while you're on my island."

Jasper boiled inside, but kept his expression neutral. "Your Majesty, with all due respect, these are my men. I'm their captain, not you. I don't want them to be disrespectful of dear Bella, but please leave the commands to me."

Peter gave Jasper a slight bow with a dangerous look. "Of course, *captain*."

Jasper addressed the crew. "As the king said, try to keep your comments lady-friendly. If you don't know what that is, ask yourself if it is something you could say around your mother."

A crewman tittered. "My mother was a bar maid. She spoke like a sailor."

Peter's nostril's flared, but before he could react, Jasper struck the comedic pirate in the face. "You knew what I meant, sailor, and you will obey!"

The group grew so quiet only the sound of waves broke into the silence. Jasper and Peter exchanged threatening looks but kept their arms at their sides.

Bella forced out, "When I imagine things, they are always colorful." She moved between Jasper and Peter. "Currently, I'm thinking of a shelter with the same colors as a whimsical circus tent."

A small cloth structure popped up before their eyes. Though it was dark, the moon illuminated the colorful striped canvas. The whole group's focus turned away from Jasper and the fae king. Several of the men gasped, and some cursed under their breath already forgetting what Jasper had told them.

Bella added excitedly, "Inside the tent would be a soft bed full of luxurious sheets and blankets. I'm hungry, so a fire with roasting meat would be right outside."

A fire pit with a wild boar on a spit appeared before their eyes. The men muttered, and Jasper cursed under his breath.

Jeb ran into the structure and called out, "Blimey, there's a bed inside the tent! Beller, are you a fairy?"

Everyone except Peter and Jasper laughed.

Peter crossed his arms. "You all can create a version of what Bella did. Go ahead and think about what you want, and it will appear. Tomorrow is going to be a long day. Having a good night's sleep is imperative."

If Jasper put Bella in charge, that might appease Peter, so Jasper took deep, calming breaths. Self-control would help him gain the advantage over losing his temper with the powerful fae. He turned to Bella.

"Would you help my men think of proper accommodations since you seem to have this figured out?"

She happily assisted those who wanted help imagining shelters, and the smell of roasted pork made everyone's mouth water. Jasper's hollow stomach grumbled. He couldn't remember his last meal. Scents of other delectable foods filled the air as each man mastered the isle's magic to transform thoughts into things.

When Jasper conjured up rum, Peter didn't balk. Maybe as long as the men didn't become drunk and disorderly, Peter didn't care about libations that added to the festive mood. As much as Jasper hated to admit it, this evening was good for the men after the typhoon. The day had taken its toll on Jasper too. His muscles ached from rowing the lifeboat, lifting his men into the vessel, and restraining his anger.

He needed music, but his lost guitar was certainly at the bottom of the sea. Focusing on his vivid memories, he called up an instrument that was identical to his original one. He almost picked it up with his hook, but grimaced when he remembered the cursed thing.

Jasper eyed the tailor and asked, "Jeb, can you play this?"

Jeb nodded. Jasper's hook almost snagged the strings as he handed it over to the sailor. Jeb put the guitar down to finish one last bite of his turkey leg. Then he wiped his hands onto his pants and grabbed the instrument.

The captain hummed a melody he knew would be appropriate, even for the uppity King Peter's standards.

"Do you know that song?"

Jeb began playing it.

Jasper drew a breath and sang, "Come lad, the ocean says to me, what adventures we'll face, oh you'll see..."

The song rambled on with the rhythm of the waves on the beach, and each sailor raised his mug in the air and joined in the chorus.

Yo ho, yo ho, me mate and I will find
Yo ho, yo ho, treasure beyond the sky.
Yo ho, yo ho, me mate and I will see
Yo ho, yo ho, how amazing it will be.

Jasper's tension gradually relaxed. As his voice blended with the other men's, he had a brief hope that the fire-haired mermaid could hear him. What if... what if he could become a merman and join Cerise? His singing stopped, though the other men continued.

Becoming a merman. Bah! Ridiculous impossibility.

Eyes drooped around the camp fire, and one by one, the men fell silent. Some yawned, and others stretched. Each man staggered to the comfortable tents, but Jasper watched Bella enter hers.

A lazy smile spread across his face. *A night with a beautiful girl would get my mind off a mermaid I can't have.*

Peter cleared his throat, pulling Jasper's attention away from Bella. "You didn't set up your own tent."

"I will sleep under the stars. I don't need a bed to feel at home as long as I'm near the sea. I feel more at home beside the ocean than any other place. I—"

Jasper stopped abruptly, mentally cursing himself. He had once admitted his love for the sea to Sven, but he no longer trusted the king to know his heart's desires. Maybe the rum had loosened his lips.

"I already knew that," the fae king said quietly. "Though you had shared your love of the sea with Sven, you'd be surprised what else I know about you." Peter's eyes changed from the violet to brown. "You may have debated on living in a nice mansion after finding treasure, but you will never be content on land. That is the biggest reason Bella isn't the girl for you."

Jasper pursed his lips. "How can you know anything about me?"

"Call it fae magic or the fact that I made it my mission to learn about you. I saw what you were planning with Bella even before you knew she existed."

A chill ran down his spine, and Jasper grunted. "How can that be. We seized your ship two years ago. I only met Bella a few weeks ago."

Peter sighed. "It's too complicated to explain tonight."

"Try."

"Do you recall that I told Bella the stories she loves are true but in a different realm?"

Jasper nodded. "Vaguely."

"I can travel to the past and future between the current timeline. I saw what you did without my intervention in the future and I had to stop you from ruining Bella." Peter rubbed his pendant. "My daughter's attempt to keep Bella safe gave you that hook. She still has plans for you, but not until I'm finished with mine."

"That's impossible." Jasper's mind was thrown into a frenzy while he absorbed what Peter had said.

"You forget, Jasper Falcon. I'm immortal. Magical time isn't the same with me. The future and past are only part of pages in a book for me. I can turn to either and visit them like an old friend." His scowl intensified. "Usually, I tend to stay out of the stories, but this time, something has forced me to become involved."

Jasper shoved himself to his feet, and his head spun. "I have no patience for your riddles. If you're not going to tell me clearly what's going on in a way that I can understand, then I'll turn in for the night. In fact, maybe I will get myself a tent to have privacy from you."

His clenched jaw was sore, and his temple throbbed from all the times he'd harnessed his anger. He dragged himself from the rest of the group to an alcove on the beach. He couldn't murder Peter, but even if he knew how to kill an immortal, he needed Peter alive.

Jasper gazed at the empty space on the beach and pictured a cabin rather than a tent. The home he left as a boy wasn't perfect, but the small house felt safe from thoughts Peter tried to manipulate. From memories Jasper didn't want to mull over. He climbed the creaky stairs to the rickety building and stumbled inside.

He wouldn't allow Peter to control the circumstances. He was his own man. He didn't need or want anyone in his life. People were either there for him to use to reach his goals or to be disposed of permanently. If he wanted Bella, he would have her.

Except, if he were honest, she wasn't what he really wanted.

What Jasper truly wished was to bring Cerise to shore.

He slammed the door on that thought. The floors groaned, but instead of feeling insecure, they brought a hint of peace, of childhood innocence. Jasper tumbled face first onto his boyhood bed, but somehow with the door shut, he felt secure.

Until the dreams invaded.

Jasper swam in the ocean to wash off the sweat from rowing before he turned in for the night. Cerise approached him shyly. The moon put a glowing halo around her head.

She touched his tattoos. "Why do you have this large falcon on your chest?"

He lifted one brow. "That, my dear, is in honor of the name I chose to escape my past and gain a reputation of a courageous bird of prey."

Cerise outlined the ocean waves that swirled around his biceps. His heart raced rapidly with her touch. "I love the water, but those represent my fight through strong waves, whether a real storm or the ones people throw at me."

The mermaid slid behind him brushed her hand over his back. Her fingers made his skin tingle until she asked, "Did you get these paintings on your back to cover your scars?"

He'd been ready to turn about, wrap her in his arms, and kiss her, but the mention of the scars stopped him. "I don't want any reminder of my parents."

Her touch vanished.

He sighed. "The Jolly Roger is part of a pirate's symbol. It's large enough to cover those old wounds, but I wanted my tattoo to be different."

"Thus, the knives instead of cross bones?"

"Yes," but the word came out in a whisper.

"Jasper," she said softly, "what do the words '*NO REGRETS AND NEVER LOOK BACK*' mean?"

He couldn't tell her they were intended for mortally wounded enemies. For a moment, he paused, searching for a believable lie. "Captain Starr forced me to get that tattoo as a reminder that I must do whatever he asked of me."

She swam around and faced him. "Jasper, where did that little innocent boy go?"

Then, she evaporated into mist.

The dream-world shifted, and Jasper was seven again, cowering in front of his drunken parents.

His dad mumbled, "Worthless boy," And his solid fist hit Jasper in the eye.

His mum spat, then said, "I should have drowned you when you were born."

The alcohol on her breath made Jasper cough. She struck him again and again. Tears stung his eyes and streamed over the bruises. Jasper broke free and darted outside, running until he could no longer see his home.

Jasper stopped, gasping for breath, at the Deptford dockyard where grand ships sailed out from London's Thames River. The sun faded below the horizon, and the bustling of crowds had died down. He was lost, but even if he knew the way home, he was too afraid to return.

He plunked down on the dock, his feet dangling over the water. Then, something bright and red caught his eye. A fin? Curiosity replaced Jasper's sorrow, and on impulse, he jumped in after the creature.

Part of him knew it was but a dream. *Foolish boy. You can't swim.*

His arms flailed and panic caused him to gulp down water. He sank. But before he went unconscious, a young girl with red hair breathed into his mouth.

Jasper coughed when he realized he was breathing water. Impossible, even in a dream, but he breathed! As the girl with long, fire-red hair and a graceful red fish-tail pulled him up from the murky depths, his vision cleared. He could see, even in the brown mirk.

Her wide, green eyes stared back at him, and she smiled. "Let me take you back to the docks."

Shocked, he couldn't reply.

Once they reached the surface, she helped him onto the quay, then climbed up after him. Her long red tail split into legs, but she didn't seem hurt by it. He looked away, then glanced back. Her long, red hair hid her body.

He coughed again, then rasped out, "What are you?"

"I'm Cerise." She tilted her head to the side and added, "I'm a mermaid."

He rubbed his eyes and stared at her.

"What's your name?" she prompted.

"Jasper."

Another smile lit her face. "That's a lovely name."

"You talk funny."

A giggle sneaked out. "My people speak a different language—"

"Like French?"

She laughed outright. "Not quite, but I enjoy hearing your words." Her gaze settled on the bruises on his face. She gently touched his cheek. "Did you get injured when you entered the water?"

He couldn't lie to her, not when she'd saved his life, so he shook his head. "No, my mum and dad did that."

Cerise's eyes grew even wider. "Oh."

Jasper stared at his hands. Maybe he shouldn't have told her?

"Jasper," she said suddenly as she placed her hand over his, "can we be friends?"

He looked up and nodded. "If... If you want. I've never met a mermaid. I thought you were only in storybooks. Your hair looks like it is on fire." His cheeks heated as the words tumbled out.

"It matches my tail," she said matter-of-factly. "Merfolk fins always match our hair."

He gulped. "I saw your tail, and that's why I jumped into the water. I thought a fish that big would be able to feed me for a long time."

Her eyes seemed sad. "Let me heal your face. I have magic, you see. Then I can get you some fish to take home."

A knot rose in Jasper's throat. He swallowed hard to ask, "Why are you helping me?"

"That's what friends do." Cerise brushed her hand over his face and sang. The pain from the blows heated and cooled.

He raised a hand, but the skin wasn't tender or sore. It was like magic. "Thank you."

She grinned. "Maybe someday you can return the favor."

"Cerise," he whispered. He smiled and touched her hair. "I love you."

Her cheeks flushed, but she only asked, "How old are you, Jasper?"

"Seven."

"I am, too! But," she added, "mermaids can live to be hundreds of years old."

"That's a long time."

"Do you live near the water?" She made a thoughtful face. "I live in the ocean, you see."

"I don't." He frowned at the water. "I was lost, before I dove in after you. I ran away from home."

She sighed.

"Oh! What if I join a ship's crew and sail the seas?"

"I don't think people allow younglings to do such grownup jobs," she said hesitantly. "But if you do, I can follow you and make sure no one harms you again. If I'm able. But that might be tricky. Mermaids belong in the sea."

"Then I belong in the sea too!"

She giggled. "Don't you mean on the sea? You can't breathe or swim under water."

"I can learn. You helped me breathe, and I've seen men swim."

"What are ye two doing here so late?"

The sudden shout startled them, and Cerise jumped into the water. Jasper called out after her, then turned to see a tall scar-faced man.

"Lad, that was a mermaid!"

"Yes, sir," Jasper said.

"You must be special," the man said slowly. "She was a wee bitty thing, but there was something different about her wild fire hair."

Jasper clamped his mouth shut. He couldn't give her away.

The man eyed him. "I overheard you say something about wanting to be a sailor. How about joining my crew?"

"I'm only seven, sir."

He chuckled. "Doesn't matter. I can teach you like my own son." The man held out a thick hand. "I'm Captain Starr, and you look like just the sort of boy I can mold into my own image."

Jasper glanced back at the maze of streets. Truthfully, he wanted to be as far from his parents as possible, but if going to sea brought him closer to Cerise? That would be even better.

"Yes, sir. I'll join your crew."

"What's your full name, boy?"

"Jasper Hook, sir, but—but—"

The man folded his arms and glared. "Well, spit it out."

"I don't want my father's name, sir. He hates me."

"Well lad, ye can decide what name suits ye best when you get older. For now, I'll call ye Jasper. Ye'll be well fed, but I'll expect you to work hard. Are ye up for the task?"

"Yes, sir!"

Dreaming Jasper wished he could call out a warning. The boy hadn't known what sort of man this Captain Starr was nor that he was leaving one kind of abuse for another.

But at least, on the ship, he was closer to the red-haired mermaid. To his truest friend.

Chapter 23

Cerise

Only slightly above the water, Cerise watched Jasper with clenched teeth as he swayed across the sand. He was near her home, but she couldn't talk to him when he had been drinking. She loathed rum that pulled Jasper deeper into piracy and away from the man she knew he could be. Her eyes welled up with tears.

Cerise loved him. She knew her feelings the first time she met him as a boy. She saw how life chipped away his goodness that only came out for her and his men. He never abused his crew unless they needed discipline and then it was only done with fairness and not cruelty, so when he kidnapped Bella, it crushed Cerise.

A crude shack popped up. King Peter must have used Jasper's thoughts to create a place to sleep. Maybe that was the home Jasper had fled as a boy, though why would he take refuge in a place that had driven him to the docks where she had first found him?

Cerise flicked her fin. Whatever the fae king had planned, she would remain close in case Jasper or Bella needed her. She knew Jasper could be a good man if given a second chance, but what would it take to prove that? She didn't want Bella scarred in the process, and Cerise had limits on how she could intervene.

She had grown up wishing to become a part of Jasper's world, yet he had told her so many years ago that he wanted to be in the ocean.

The thought made her pause, *Could Peter turn him into a merman?*

Her heart fluttered at the thought, but then she shook her head. At the moment, Jasper was too obsessed with treasure. Merfolk had their own kind of riches, but it wasn't what humans deemed valuable.

Still, a mergirl could wish upon a sea star for her true love to be in her world.

So, while Jasper slumbered in the rickety hut Peter had conjured for him, she waited and hoped. A song sprung from her joy at the possibilities.

The bonny boy so sweet and free
Will join me someday in the sea.
He'll leave his pain and past behind
In hopes of his true love to find.

Chapter 24

Jasper

Intense sunlight cut through the tattered curtains and flared its rays into Jasper's eyes. He grunted, annoyed at the disturbance. The glinting light made his headache worse. The bittersweet memory of Cerise's arrival didn't lift his mood.

He propped himself up on his right elbow and scanned his surroundings. What on earth—or on an Ageless Isle—had made him create *this* place? Why hadn't he thought of a mansion or something better?

Running away and changing his name and future should have permanently erased those unwanted memories. The fae king must have read his mind to revert him to that feeble little boy who hid in a dirty, dilapidated cabin—the only place he could call home before the *Black Fear*.

Jasper fisted his hands. Peter was not allowed to wiggle inside his head again. Ignoring the shirt he'd pulled off before falling asleep, Jasper shoved himself to his feet. The decrepit floors creaked and wobbled when he crossed them. The warm morning light felt good on his bare back. He shaded his eyes to look up the beach. There wasn't a person in sight.

Bella's tent was obvious. The colorful monstrosity of red, white, blue, and purple stripes made Jasper's eyes throb, and rather than cheering him, the thing made him nauseous. Of course, the strange girl who loved books more than real life would have thought up something so outlandish.

Each of the other tents, however, displayed the crew's individual personalities, which gave Jasper pause. How could a world that had such magic also have limitations? Perhaps King Peter wasn't totally upfront with them.

Perhaps he had manipulated this whole thing from the start.

Maybe even the ship where they found Sven after killing everyone else was an illusion? If that was the case, Peter could certainly craft a vessel to carry all the crew and treasure from Ageless Isle to the Caribbean. Jasper raked his fingers through his hair absentmindedly. He had lost treasure to the storm, but now he could replenish it ten-fold. His frown turned into a grin.

He had only to confront the illustrious fae king and convince him to...

But none of the tents were fancy enough to fit Peter's loftiness. Jasper counted the structures. There weren't enough to hold each of the crew plus Bella and Peter.

Suddenly, Jasper's anger boiled. He barged into Bella's tent. "Where is he?"

Bella blinked groggily at him, then gasped, grabbed the colorful blankets, and pulled them over her body. "What are you doing here?"

There was no one else in the bed.

"King Peter doesn't have his own tent." Jasper glared at the girl. "I thought perhaps he had joined you."

Her brows knitted together, and her cheeks flushed.

"That's despicable! He's like a father to me. Did you rudely search all the tents or just jump to a nasty conclusion?"

"No, but I counted them, and there aren't enough for Peter to have his own." Jasper's breathing steadied. "I seriously doubt his majesty would sleep with one of the other men."

"Why wouldn't he? He has before when he was Sven."

"True, but he was playing a part. Why would a king bunk with commoners when he doesn't have to?"

Bella rolled her eyes. "Let me get properly dressed, and I will help you find him."

Jasper's gaze roamed over Bella's face and mussed hair.

She glared back at him but didn't make a move.

"Oh, you want me to leave your tent? That seems extreme," he said. "Aren't you wearing the same clothes as yesterday."

"No." She shot eye-daggers at him. "Just like I imagined the tent, I thought of something more comfortable for sleeping."

The idea hadn't crossed Jasper's mind, and he found himself wishing he had conjured up different clothes.

"What do you think you are doing in here?"

Peter's rumbled question caught Jasper by surprise, and he spun around to face the king. "I was looking for you."

Peter narrowed his eyes. "Here I am. You can leave her alone."

"I'm curious," Jasper tried to cross his arms, but the cursed hook got in the way. Instead, he raised his chin. "Why are you so worried about Miss Bonnay's virtue?"

"If you have to ask, then you are definitely not the man for her."

Jasper clenched his fist and pivoted on his heels. He walked briskly out of Bella's sleeping quarters, not-so-accidentally shoving into Peter with his shoulder as he passed. Peter stood his ground, murmured a pleasantry to Bella, then followed the captain into the sunlight. Jasper silently counted to ten to calm his mental images of thrashing the fae.

"Where were you?" Jasper growled.

"I was in Jeb's tent. I didn't see the need to create a new one since I have been sharing quarters with the crew for a while now. Why did you think I would be with Bella?"

"Because you're so worried about protecting her from nasty pirates." If he figured out Peter's angle, maybe Jasper could use it against the fae later on. "Why exactly does the king of the fae want to protect Bella?"

"I have my reasons, but you don't need to know them."

"Then get me off this blasted island."

Peter smirked. "I can't do that just yet. Also, I didn't say you couldn't gather treasure from here?"

"Yes, but you pointed out, that it would be hard to transport anything to another port without a ship. And you said something about the inhabitants not being too keen on humans."

"True, although a brave pirate captain wouldn't care about dangerous creatures." Peter pointed upward beyond their view. "Besides, with the right amount of concentration, you could create another *Black Fear* for your remaining crew to return to the human realm even if you will need my help to get back there." He made a point to look at Jasper's rundown cabin. "I see you came up with a rather odd choice for a place to sleep last night."

Jasper's jaw tightened.

The fae glowered. "But then, if you applied your mind to the situation, you could think up something better to wear than what you have on."

Jasper stepped toe-to-toe with Peter, his nose inches from the king's. "Why do you care what I wear?"

Peter's nostrils flared, but the fae held his ground. "I care that your lack of attire makes Bella uncomfortable. And you will never be good enough for her."

"Why do you care so much about Bella?" Jasper scoffed.

Peter pivoted and walked away without giving Jasper an explanation. Jasper watched him through narrowed eyes. It seemed important to the king that Bella remained unmarred by pirates, and while Jasper didn't understand the fae's motives, he resented Peter's games.

Jasper straightened and waved a dismissive hand. What he truly needed to know was whether or not he could leave this island with the fortune Sven had promised. If he couldn't, he would have to escape, then commandeer another ship and win back his booty using old-fashioned pirate methods.

Jasper took in his surroundings. On one side, the beach met the beautiful cerulean sea. To the other, unclimbable white cliffs rose. Maybe that was the real reason Peter had told them to make camp for the night. How were they going to get up the vertical precipices?

Yawns and grumbles caught Jasper's attention. One by one, the odorous pirates gathered around him.

Jeb sidled up to Jasper and whispered, "Wha' riled up Petah this mornin'? He stomped ow of me tent like his pants was on fire."

"He was worried I was going to sully Bella's virtue." Jasper studied the younger pirate. "I don't mind if you call him Peter, just don't do it around him. I don't trust him, and neither should you. The best thing to do is play along with what he wants until we can escape his clutches."

"Don' wurry, Cap'n," the tailor protested. "The king won't 'arm us."

"Don't underestimate him, Jeb. That fae has magical abilities. Also, I suspect he can read my mind based on the things he says. If you have thoughts you don't want him to know, I'd keep them out of your head."

Jeb chuckled. "I rarely fink, Cap'n so that won' be a problem."

Jasper shook his head. Captain Starr's many rules had been *"Trust no one but yourself because outside influences can distort your judgement if you're not careful."* The memory made Jasper smirk. Starr had forgotten to follow his own rules.

"You're not a total idiot," he told the tailor after a glance in Peter's direction, "but you're too trusting. Don't let your fondness for Sven blind your judgment."

Jeb nodded just as the king swiped his arms in the air. The tents and Jasper's shabby cabin vanished.

Jasper frowned and called out, "If you can do all that, is it possible to clean us up a little? Between the sea, campfire, and rum, my men stink."

Peter's nose wrinkled. "You don't smell like a rose, either. Yes, I will, if only because Bella should not have to tolerate the stench."

He snapped his fingers. Jasper not only smelled clean, but he also wore his crimson waistcoat, a crisp white linen shirt, and black breeches. A sword exactly like the one Quinn had made hung from a leather belt on his right side, and slick black boots Jasper had lost at sea covered his feet. The hidden knife remained under his new trousers sheathed around his left leg.

"I knew it! You can do more magic than you let on. But," Jasper conceded, "I see that traveling last night would have been impossible. How are we supposed to get over that cliff?"

Peter arced a brow. "With the help of Tilly and some happy thoughts."

"Bah! That's absurd." Jasper widened his stance and waved his hook at the steep cliffs. "Can't you move us all up there with a snap of your fingers the same way you gave me new clothes?"

The scent of roses accompanied Bella as she walked over and joined their conversation. Lines between her brows formed and she tilted her head.

"Something about this seems vaguely familiar. I believe that there was something about happy thoughts and pixie dust in a story, but it is foggy. I can't recall the details."

A scowl flashed across Peter's face, but other than not wanting to talk about Bella's ridiculous stories again, Jasper couldn't see what could have offended the fae king.

"Here on Ageless Isle," Peter said, "we can fly with the magic of pixie dust and happy thoughts. I don't know how else to explain it in simpler terms."

Jeb and Will exchanged doubtful glances, and Jasper silently agreed. Happy thoughts carrying them up the cliff?

Ridiculous.

The king mumbled the incantation he had used when they were stalked by the shark of which "Tilly" was the only word Jasper recognized.

A speck of light raced toward them, and the miniature fairy bowed in mid-air. "What do you need, Your Majesty?"

"We need to get everyone up the cliff. Since climbing is out of the question, could you give us some more pixie dust?"

Tilly tapped her miniature chin with her forefinger. "For you I will, but we don't like strangers on our island. Why did you bring them here anyway?"

"I have my reasons." Peter glared around the circle of stranded pirates. "And they will be on their best behavior. Or else."

Steam was going to come out of Jasper's ears like from a boiling kettle. This was *Sven*, his first mate, talking in this superior way. Jasper was the captain, not Peter, and the unwelcome thought drifted in:

Would leaving the shore open up Jasper for more humiliation? The longer he spent in the lying, former first officer's presence, the less tempting the rumored riches seemed. Maybe they should look for a way to get off the blasted island instead.

"The tricky part about pixie dust is that it doesn't always work on humans," Peter was saying. "It can move objects with ease, but humans also need to believe they can fly." He tapped his temple. "Try to empty your mind of all the negative thoughts and focus on something that makes you truly happy."

The crew chuckled like naughty school boys getting away with something. Bella's face scrunched in concentration. Jasper squinted in an attempt to block out everything but something pleasant.

"Some of you have had horrible pasts, but grab a memory that really made you happy or maybe think of something you wish you could have—" Peter glanced over at Bella. "—a happily ever after, if it were written in a book."

The girl seemed to be struggling to think of something pleasant as much as Jasper was. Peaceful nights at sea had always given him solace. He focused on the way the ocean lulled him to sleep and how the salt water seemed to be part of his blood. Life on the sea had been nearly blissful after he got rid of Captain Starr.

Then his mind drifted to Cerise. Her emerald eyes and fire-blazoned hair were tattooed on his memory. If he could live in the sea with her, that would be his true happiness, but he shook the thought away. Peter wanted them to think of something real or could come true, and being with Cerise was a fairy tale like the ones Bella read. He forced all his thoughts on the sea and how it made him feel.

Tilly flew over them, blowing sparkly dust on their heads.

Sneezes echoed against the cliffs when several pirates inhaled the powder.

Everyone except Jasper and Bella seemed to have thought of something worthy of flying because soon the men were floating above the sandy shore. The king positioned his body in a horizontal pose like a bird and began flying upward toward the top of the cliffs.

When Jasper's thoughts strayed back to Cerise, he began to drift upward, leaving Bella behind, which confused him. Her previous wealthy life had to be full of happy moments.

He softly landed besides his crew on the clifftop which was covered by a cushion of green vegetation with an earthen, mossy smell. Before they wandered farther inland, Jasper glanced back to the edge for one last time.

A gentle ocean breeze as soft as a woman's caress brushed over his skin. The beautiful, azure water was calm and clear—the exact opposite of the day before, when he'd lost the *Black Fear*. Somehow, despite the loss, his heart soared knowing Cerise was real.

He'd lost his ship and already missed his beloved sea, but it wasn't over. He would find his way back and leave this land with or without its treasures.

Chapter 25

Bellarose

B ella's thoughts whirled, and she squeezed her eyes shut in concentration. Sweat beaded on her neck. The creativity to invent a tent and a dress didn't require happiness, but conjuring up a joyful thought powerful enough to make her fly was daunting. Her recent months had been more of a nightmare than a joy.

Except for Quinn.

Finding someone she could love deeply and to have that affection returned would be the happiest ending anyone could ask for in the world. True, he didn't join the *Black Fear*, but thinking of his smile made her all mushy inside. If she loved him as much as she thought she might... Her heart beat faster.

Whenever she expected something in return for kindness, it left an empty hole inside. Her true joy came when she gave without expectations. As she had helped Quinn, she felt whole, and in turn, he did much more for her.

Her focus must have been enough because, light as a feather, she rose above the shore. Loose hair brushed her face, and her muscles relaxed as she effortlessly flew to the top of the cliff only a minute behind Jasper. Bella's insides tingled, even though she grew a little shaky when she glanced at the shrinking golden shoreline and rolling waves. Fortunately, she landed on her feet before panic hit.

Dark green clover and moss carpeted the clifftop. She glanced behind her. They had bounced back to their original shapes as she joined the others.

Only the distant ocean waves and the songs of exotic birds made noise. The men seemed to have lost their usually hinged tongues. If the overwhelming feeling of awe made a sound, there would have been a cacophony rolling off the pirates.

Peter was the first to speak. "Come. We have a lot of walking to do. It would be best to keep up with me."

Bella didn't hesitate, but Jasper and his men looked skeptical. They eyed Peter and then the ocean beyond the cliffs. She motioned for them to follow but couldn't blame them for second-guessing the best course of action. After all, nothing about Ageless Isle seemed normal. There might be unexpected dangers only the king could anticipate, but. Sven-Peter hadn't been honest with them. There was no guarantee that he had any of their best interests in mind.

Bella wanted to trust him but wasn't entirely sure Peter was safe. She had seen what his daughter could do when provoked. What if Peter decided they were all a waste of his time and put a hex on them? It might not be probable, but it was a possibility, wasn't it?

The farther they moved away from the cliffs, the denser the vegetation became. Soon they were in a forest with trees so tall that Bella could see neither their tops nor around their vast trunks. The massive trees blocked the sun, making it feel like late afternoon instead of morning.

The air grew cool under the trees' thick foliage, and the fragrance of cedar hit Bella's nose. When she wished for a cloak to take away the chill, one sprang from mid-air and draped itself around her shoulders, but no one else seemed to notice the new dark-tan garment's sudden appearance.

Occasionally, the ancient trunks would creak and groan, but sometimes Bella thought she heard giggling children and rustling noises in the underbrush. Perhaps smaller woodland creatures were scurrying to escape the strangers. Goosebumps rose on her arms.

I must reign in my imagination.

Then, without warning, a scream shattered the peaceful forest.

"Huzzooee!"

A boy clad in colorful patch-work clothing swung from a rope between two trees.

"Huzzooee!" multiple voices screamed in unison.

More boys in similar clothing appeared and hung upside-down from the trees to drop nets over the adults. Stopped in their tracks, the group huddled under the trap. A lanky boy with spiked blond hair stepped directly in front of their rope prison. The boy stationed himself in front of Bella and stared her straight in the eye. She wasn't tall, but knowing his height didn't help her figure out how old he was. Something about him seemed... timeless?

"Unwelcome to Ageless Isle." He offered them all an insincere, toothy grin. "If you don't leave, we'll cut out your throats."

"What gives you the power or right to threaten our lives, boy?" Jasper growled.

"The obvious fact that you are trapped."

"King Peter," Bella cried, but when there was no answer, she twisted under the net looking for the king. He had been leading them. He should have been the one handling the strange boys. But she couldn't see him. "Where is the king?"

"King Peter left you to your fate." The boy rubbed his hands together gleefully. "You're our prisoners and must pass our tests to stay on the island, even if we'd rather you leave. Either way, we can cut your throats if you don't cooperate."

Jasper laughed loudly. "Bah! You're only a boy!"

Bella cringed at Jasper's lack of fear. This *boy* threatened to kill them.

"You can laugh all you want, but you won't think it's funny when your blood is covering the ground. Do what I say, and maybe, just maybe, your lives will be spared."

Between clenched teeth Bella hissed, "Jasper, you're not helping us." Then, she smiled brightly at the boy. "What's your name?"

"Jericho, and I'm the leader of the forest leprechauns."

"What in bloody h—"

Bella elbowed Jasper. When he yelped, she scowled and jabbed him again.

"What is a leprechaun?" Jasper finished, his words dripping with suspicion. "You look more like a boy, who certainly couldn't beat me in a sword fight."

Bella groaned. That pirate was going to get them all in trouble.

"I've read stories about leprechauns." Bella focused on putting a pleasant lilt in her voice. "And you don't exactly fit the description."

Jasper rolled his eyes and muttered, "Of course you have."

"Who might you be, miss?" Jericho squinted at Bella.

"I'm Bella, and this is Captain Jasper Falcon of the *Black Fear* and his crew."

"Well, Bella," the boy said with a hint of arrogance, "I don't know about your stories, but we are leprechauns—the mightiest warriors of the fae folk on the island. And I assure you, Captain Falcon, size will not matter if you decide to fight us."

Even though these boys didn't seem as dangerous as their threats, diplomacy was better than bullying, which seemed to be Jasper's only strategy.

Jasper heaved a deep sigh. "What test must we pass?"

"We can't show you here, but if you agree to take it, then we won't kill you now."

"Do we all have to pass it or only one of us?" Bella asked politely.

Jericho's gray eyes stared at Jasper. "He definitely has to pass the test, but maybe you, my lady, could get off with telling us one of those stories you mentioned." Jericho grinned at Bella and then motioned to the other boys. "Lads, take this group to our testing arena."

The netting magically disappeared, and each pirate was bound by their wrists and attached to the nearest crewmate, though Bella was left unbound. The ropes were made of vines, but when the men struggled to break free of them, the bindings tightened.

"I'd be careful not to struggle too hard," one of the boys said. "That rope will cut off your circulation if you keep pulling on it. It only strengthens when it feels resistance. It will loosen a little if you give up trying to escape."

All the men stopped fighting. Even Jasper, who was at the front of the line, cooperated.

Jericho and his boys—or rather leprechauns—yanked the ropes and dragged the pirates forward pushing and prodding the men with wooden spears out of what seemed like spite. Bella walked next to Jericho, and the lad looped her arm into his.

"Bella, we have many beautiful creatures on this island—mermaids, pixies, and our enchantress—and I never thought a nasty human could compare. You definitely have your own kind of beauty." He leaned closer and whispered in her ear, "Before he left, the king told us to keep Jasper away from you. We can definitely do that."

Although Jericho and the others weren't as tiny as leprechauns she'd read about and they definitely didn't look as threatening as they claimed to be, a shiver ran down her back all the same. Magic would give them the upper hand, even over the cutthroat pirates. Maybe Jasper had finally met his match.

Chapter 26

Jasper

Jasper's head throbbed with frustration that once again, Peter had managed to control him. Those boys and their threats were no match for a pirate captain, but until he could be free from their blasted traps, he couldn't kill the whole lot of them.

Gradually, a musical noise began to compete with the forest's quiet sounds. Was that water?

The leprechauns led Jasper, Bella, and the crew to a wide clearing, and Jasper gasped in awe. Amidst the open space, sunlight sparkled on a turquoise lake. In the middle of the expanse of water, mermaids basked on a gigantic, flat rock. Though he had only seen her in the ocean, Jasper squinted to see if Cerise was amongst the group, but the waterfall behind them caught his eye.

Light shimmered off the water, making it appear as if diamonds were tumbling inside the stream.

Treasure... The thought diverted his focus from the mermaids, and he blinked several times. "Am I imagining sapphires, rubies, and emeralds within those falls?"

"Your eyes aren't deceiving you," Jericho said. "This is Treasure Lagoon. Those are gems of the most valuable kind, but there is a trick to retrieving the nuggets."

"That's another answer that doesn't explain anything at all." When the boy didn't clarify, Jasper sighed heavily. "Fine. What kind of trick?"

"The kind that will be your trial to stay on the island." The boy smirked, "Captain, this lagoon is your test arena."

One of the pirates snorted, and a glance back showed Jasper that his men were gaping at the fish women like school boys.

Jasper grumbled inwardly, but his mood changed when he noticed Cerise. Here? In the center of an island? Mermaids must have had magic that allowed them to travel between bodies of water or else there must have been a secret passageway through the waterfall to the ocean. Either way she was a sight for irritated eyes.

"The mermaids are protective of their treasure trove," Jericho said pulling Jasper's attention from the red-headed mermaid. "Though they are lovely to look upon, they are as deadly as forest leprechauns."

Jasper couldn't help it. He laughed. The noise startled the birds from trees.

"You expect me to believe those lovely maidens would cut our throats? That is the most hilarious thing I've heard today." He wiped a make-believe tear from his eye. "It's one thing for you to expect me to believe that you boys can kill me in a fight, but those creatures look about as capable of murder as Bella here. And she is pretty much helpless, despite her bravado."

Jericho wagged his index figure in the air. "Tsk, tsk, tsk, Captain Falcon. You have too much confidence in your strength and size. Muscles do not make you a worthy adversary for any of the inhabitants of Ageless Isle. The sooner you accept that, the longer you will live. Those mermaids' teeth are sharper than any knife you'll ever own. They could tear your throats to shreds as easily as if they were a large bear."

"Is that a clue? Are you telling me what test I need to pass to stay on the island?"

Jericho gave Jasper a sinister smile. "Not today. Tonight, you'll be our guests, and then tomorrow, you will die."

The boys dragged the men past the lagoon to a grove. Every imaginable fruit and some Jasper didn't recognize hung from the trees. Colorful blossoms covered other branches, and the scent was exquisite.

The men tramped past citrus trees, and the tang of lemons and oranges gave way to sweet apples and plums, but some of the exotic fruit smells made him sneeze and called to mind the spicy Spanish dishes he tasted once. He had the sudden urge to drink something cool and wash away the burn that wasn't truly there.

Bella seemed fascinated by the trees as well. She pointed at an unusual cluster of fruit. "Jericho? What are these?"

"Cinnapepper trees."

"I've never heard of them before."

"They only grow here. The fruit tastes like cinnamon and pepper, and most of us use it for seasoning food rather than eating. We sometimes dare a youngling to bite into one, and literally smoke comes out of his ears." Jericho and a few of the other boys laughed.

Bella tripped over a root, but Jericho kept her from falling.

"Thank you." She straightened wiggled her foot before leaning on it. She wasn't injured for she only asked, "How old are you?"

Jericho scratched his chin. "I guess if I didn't live on Ageless Isle, I'd be fifty-five, but I arrived here when I was fifteen."

Bella glanced around the group. "Are there only male leprechauns?"

His forehead wrinkled. "That's a strange question to ask, but yes."

"Where did you all come from?"

Did the girl ever fall silent? Still, whether she meant to help or not, gathering information on the boys might be useful.

"Miss Bella, you are full of questions." Jericho exhaled. "Anyway, we're foundlings from other worlds. We wished upon a star for a life away from the orphanage or streets. The pixies heard our wishes and brought us here to become forest leprechauns."

"Aren't there any girl orphans wishing for escape?" Bella asked.

"There are, but they become pixies."

Interesting. Jasper's curiosity was perked. Maybe there was more to be gained here than simple jewels. He tried to get closer to Jericho and Bella and in doing so yanked on the pirate tied to his arm.

"Did you say you don't age?"

Jericho grinned maliciously.

"The same magic that keeps us youthful gives us the ability to kill you with little effort."

"Then I should be able to access that magic, too."

Jericho laughed and shook his head. "No, not until you pass the test. We all have to prevail over the lagoon's trials, or we die."

Bella gasped.

Torn between inquisitiveness and disbelief, Jasper asked, "What happens if we succeed?"

"If you don't fail, you can stay ad use the island's magic."

The group maneuvered over protruding roots and passed some rotting tree stumps surrounded by mushrooms. The pirates grumbled but didn't join the conversation. Good. Jasper's guess was that they were assessing the situation for the chance to escape, just as he had trained them to do if they were captured. Although... The other leprechauns may have been sizing up the pirates, too, since only Jericho spoke.

While the idea of living here forever with people like Jericho or Peter turned Jasper's stomach, but magic and immortality? He wouldn't mind that. From the day he left his home and joined the pirates, he worked toward obtaining wealth, but now that he knew Cerise was real, riches weren't enough. Perhaps this isle could give him the ability to turn into a merman? All he had to do was pass the boys' imbecilic test, and perhaps he could have his heart's desire after all.

Chapter 27

Bellarose

During the walk, Bella had observed her surroundings and asked question after question, trying to determine whom she could trust and if she could leave the island without magical assistance. Every time her bookworm side got distracted by the fantastical fairy tale elements or thoughts of conversations she'd have with Quinn if he was there, Bella dug her fingernails into her palms to keep her focused.

The leprechauns' village was exactly the epitome of a place where boys who never grew up would live. Ladders took them up to treehouses which were as mismatched as their clothing was.

The houses encircled a large, round table with rickety chairs. Ramps and planks connected the trees around the sitting area.

Bella frowned. If the boys ate at the table, they wouldn't be protected from showers or bad weather. Maybe they ate in drizzle. Or maybe it didn't rain here.

Jericho motioned to the table. "Sit down and get ready to eat a feast larger than any you've ever had."

Before taking a seat, Bella scanned the area for Peter, but he was nowhere to be seen. Her one consolation was that he must know the leprechauns wouldn't hurt her since it seemed that he had left her with them.

Several boys brought out dinner plates and large, empty platters, though Bella didn't see a kitchen. The boys, however, sat and began to chomp and gulp down air in obvious delight.

Bella and Jasper's sparse crew exchanged glances. One pirate made a circular motion near his temple with one finger and mouthed, "Crazy."

Jericho said, with what sounded like a full mouth, "Sit! Eat!"

They obeyed the command to sit, but how could they eat what wasn't there?

Jericho stopped chewing. "Isn't our food good enough for you?"

Bella glanced at the others. Jasper's mouth was tight as he glared at the boys. Since no one else spoke, she replied tentatively, "There isn't any food."

The leprechauns guffawed, and Jericho waved a hand to stop them.

"You must believe there is food. It will appear with the right imagination."

Beside Bella, Jasper cursed under his breath, then said for all to hear, "Is everything on this island created by imagination?"

"Just about. That's why it's tricky for the average grown-up to live here." Jericho took a sip from his apparently empty cup and smirked at Jasper. "Or take anything away from the island. If they pass our test and don't die—which most of them do—they don't have enough imagination to keep the treasures from disappearing when they leave."

"You've gots to believe," a boy with floppy, brown hair yelled.

Before Jasper could start arguing again, Bella turned to the outspoken lad. "And who are you?"

"I'm Barney, and I's got lots of 'magination. Right now..." He chomped at the air next to his closed fist, chewed, and gulped. His words were muffled when he explained, "I'm eating a huge turkey leg."

Bella chewed her lower lip. "Are you all eating the same thing, or do you get what you think about?"

"All different," Barney replied around a mouthful of nothing.

Jasper huffed. "Bah! That's the most ridiculous thing I've ever heard."

"I don't know," Bella said. "We did the same sort of thing on the beach when our tents and food appeared. Maybe this isn't so unbelievable."

Jasper scowled and folded his arms—though he was obviously careful not to snag his crimson vest with his hook.

"Well, I'm going to try it," she said. Again, she closed her eyes and imagined.

When she peeked, the most delectable pile of mashed potatoes and gravy appeared. Picking up a silver fork, she began to eat. She hadn't realized how hungry she really was.

Once her own food blinked into existence, she could see what each person was eating. One boy had a plate full of cookies. She judged that wouldn't be satisfying or healthy, but then, she hadn't created any green vegetables, either. Around the table, the pirates followed her lead, and roasted chicken, potatoes, and pies appeared on each plate.

Jasper's remained empty, and she almost felt sorry for his stubbornness.

"Jasper, you need to think of something you like. Anything! It will appear, and you'll see the delightful things all of us are eating,"

She stopped herself. What was she doing, encouraging him? Such a cruel person didn't deserve her sympathy.

"This is all balderdash. You want me to believe that you're actually eating real food? If it is produced by some mind power, can it satisfy? Or are your head creations so great you'll get full from your make-believe food?"

Bella wiped her hands on a napkin. "Why is it so hard to accept? We did it before at the beach. You even conjured up rum."

"We could care less if you starve, but listen to the lady." Jericho clicked his tongue. "The only foolish one right now is you."

Faster than Bella could comprehend, Jasper grabbed her. His hook pressed against her waist, and he held a knife at her throat. "I'm tired of these games! Give me what I want, or Bella dies."

Bella's fork clanked loudly onto the table along with several other utensils. The mashed potatoes crashed like rocks in her stomach, but Bella didn't even squeak. What had Quinn taught her if she were in a situation like this? Panic erased his lessons. Only mouth breathers and forest creatures could be heard as the pirates sat in silence watching the scene unfold in real time.

Out of nowhere, a vine wrapped around Jasper's throat. It whipped into a hangman's noose. He released her and dropped the knife.

Jericho jumped out of his seat and bound Jasper in more vines.

In minutes, the leprechauns dragged the captain to a makeshift cage made out of sticks and tree branches. They locked it with a metal padlock and hoisted it up in the air. The vine let Jasper go, and he coughed.

Bella drew a deep breath and fingered her throat. Her hands shook. *Leave it to Jasper to skip eating and go right to violence.*

"You almost killed me!" Jasper croaked.

"You threatened Bella," Jericho screamed.

The pirate didn't back down. "You promised me a test before you killed me."

"After the feast, but you chose to skip that part. That's fine by me. I don't like rude table guests anyway."

That attack in the cabin had been frightening, but a knife to her throat and a hook pressing against her stomach? She almost preferred the captain's seduction to his violence.

Why hadn't the hex on his hook pull it away the second he tried to harm her? It was almost as if the spell knew he wouldn't succeed.

"Keep eating." Jericho ordered. "Don't let that fool ruin our feast. Tomorrow, all of you will have to take the test. You need your strength." He gave Bella a large grin. "Tonight, Bella will perform her trial. She will tell us a tale of the leprechauns she read about in books."

Jasper hung in the mid-air jail. The pirates continued their meals, albeit more slowly than before. Jeb faltered whenever he eyed his captain.

Bella managed to finish her potatoes, then raised her voice. "Once upon a time a man from America decided to visit Ireland."

"What's America?" asked a brown-haired boy.

"Shh," hushed the others.

All eyes were fixed on her. "It's a country. Now this American wasn't a believer of magic or fantastical creatures, but soon, he found a leprechaun family living in the cottage where he was staying. The leprechauns were wee people, no larger than the palm of the man's hands."

Barney blurted out, "We're bigger than that!"

Jericho eyed him and he closed his lips and held them together with his fingers.

Bella continued with the story. "When the American met an Irish girl, his own story intermingled with the leprechaun's."

She told them about how the daughter from the king of the fairies and the son of the leprechaun's leader fell in love and the war between the fairies and leprechauns, spinning the tale of star-crossed lovers. She went on.

How the humans helped stop the battle so the world wouldn't crumble. Bella weaved between battle scenes and the love story, and when the tale ended, Jeb was crying, and Barney and Will applauded. Jasper, of course, only made snarky comments under his breath.

One boy stood up and whistled, and another called out, "Bella, that was great!"

Jericho bowed to her. "It was totally wrong about us leprechauns, but you definitely passed your test. You can stay."

"As if King Peter would have allowed you to kill her if she didn't pass your idiotic trial," Jasper spat out. He took a swig from a bottle. He might not have been able to conjure food, but evidently rum was within the scope of his imagination.

Bella grimaced. His belligerence only made him more pathetic.

Jericho glared at Jasper. "You need to keep your mouth shut. You'll need your strength tomorrow, Captain Falcon, so you may want to eat more than you drink."

The boy—or leprechaun—clapped his hands together. "Let us all go to sleep. Leprechaun lads, show the pirates to their beds. Bella, follow me."

She climbed up the stairs to planks that led to more stairs and then a ladder that climbed to one of the larger treehouses. Jericho opened the door to the little enclosed cottage, and she saw a big bed with a smaller cot off to the side.

"I will sleep outside the cottage." He folded up the cot to move it. "King Peter wants me to keep you safe from the forest creatures and pirates."

"Forest creatures?" She shot a nervous look at the door. "Should I be worried? What kind of dangers are out there besides you and your lads?"

"Redcaps and voldermice, mostly."

Bella hid a yawn. "I've heard of the redcap fairies. Don't they kill for fun and soak their caps with the blood of their victims?"

He nodded. "But don't worry. They won't harm us because of a pact King Peter made with them long ago, though humans who find the isle are fair game unless they pass our trial."

"I passed, so wouldn't the redcaps leave me alone?"

"Not until you've gone through the ceremony to make it official, which will happen after your whole crew finishes their exam," he explained. "Tonight, you are safe as our guests, but I like to take precautions. Tomorrow, it's everyone for himself."

She bit her lip. "And what are the voldermice?"

"They look like normal mice, but then change into venomous snakes and kill you with one bite," he said with a degree of enthusiasm completely out of place for something so frightening. "They stay away from our tree houses, though, because we coated the bark with something that smells like cats. That's enough to keep them away. But like I said, don't worry. I'll keep an eye out. You'll be safe."

"I have so many questions about this island and its inhabitants, but I'm—" Bella couldn't stop the yawn "—tired."

"Yes, it's time to sleep, for tomorrow some of you may die." He chuckled.

"That's horrible," Bella began, but fatigue dragged her into a dreamless sleep before she could finish.

Chapter 28

Jasper

J asper woke suddenly. Far below, the burning campfire still crackled brightly, warming his cage.

His stomach growled, and he swallowed his pride and conjured some food, then weapons. Even if he passed the test, whatever it would be, he trusted neither Peter nor the boys who had imprisoned him. He finished his bread and cheese, then tried to break out of the wooden jail with a saw, but the branches must have been magically protected. He gave up his escape attempt and tried to settle in the uncomfortable cage.

Unable to keep his eyes open, Jasper dozed. Disturbing dreams and an awful, tangy stench woke him. Warm, odorous air blew into his face. He jerked upright, A tiny, bearded man with beady-eyes and claw-like fingers clung to the outside of the prison. The wee man wore a dripping, red bonnet. Jasper knew that coppery smell: the cap was saturated in blood.

A sharp blade reflected the firelight. The tiny man hissed roughly, "I'll get your blood for me cap, and you will be in a forever nap."

Jasper rapidly pulled out his own weapon, but another voice behind him whispered, "His blood is for me cap, you sap!"

Redcap fae.

His heart raced. His mum had told him they would kill him in his sleep if he was a bad boy.

His arms trembled, and his fingers curled around his knife's handle. He could take them in a knife fight—

Unless they were like the so-called leprechauns.

And unless they have magic.

Jasper rose to a crouch. "You won't be getting any of my blood tonight!"

"Huzzooee!"

Two leprechauns appeared out of nowhere. Their blades sliced through the redcaps, which dropped into the fire. The scent of burnt flesh temporarily filled the air.

Jasper gaped. First, they lock him up for threatening Bella, now they save his life?

"The pact protects our camp," a wild-eyed boy sang, "and your jail is part of our camp."

"What do you mean?" Jasper asked.

"Never you mind," the boy said. "You'd best sleep. No beasties will harm you tonight."

"Huzzooee!" the boy named Barney yelled.

The leprechauns disappeared as quickly as they had appeared.

Eventually, the day's events caught up and Jasper's eye-lids grew too heavy to keep open. He couldn't stay awake.

Chapter 29

Peter

Aerowyn had been home when Peter left the humans in the forest. She had already fetched their customary cups and a pot of fae tea, and the cursed wolf, Gerard, sat on a cushion at her side.

"Daughter," he exclaimed.

She rose to greet him, and as she poured the steaming liquid, she explained her plans for Jasper. "And you weren't supposed to be on the *Black Fear* in the first place, Father. Jasper is my project."

"I know and that's why I used our mind connection for you to go to New Orleans sooner," he said. "But Bella is mine, and I was rightfully concerned that she needed more protection than you had planned."

Aerowyn frowned. Beside her, Gerard's ears flattened slightly. "Father, it was you who wanted me to rid the world of villains. Jasper is one of many, and his terror upon the seas needs to end. I'm only fulfilling the mission you started after we moved to Ageless Isle."

"I know, I know, but Jasper is so foul." Peter rubbed his palms together. "Reading his thoughts made me feel like I needed to scour my mind. He has done some truly awful things, and before you gave him that hooked hand, he treated women deplorably."

Aerowyn looked down. "Exactly, and that's why he needs the same treatment we've given all the others—curse, lesson, then choice to break the hex for redemption."

Gerard growled.

"It seems that your wolf and I disagree with you. I don't think he deserves the chance to change. He should have that cursed hook until he dies, which he will do soon enough."

Aerowyn's eyes widened. "Father! Everyone should be given a chance at redemption. If they reject the opportunity, then that is their choice. You saw his childhood. You know how it molded him."

Peter sipped his tea. "Many humans have experienced similar abuse—or worse—without becoming evil."

A single tear trickled down her cheek. "You of all people should understand how easy it is to make bad decisions based on your own pain."

The words were a punch in the stomach. He closed his eyes and leaned back. "You speak the truth."

How easy it was to forget his own flaws when he was too busy examining other's iniquities. When Peter had cursed Callista, she used the magic he had gifted her and summoned the tempest that had killed both of Jasper's grandfathers at sea. The result of their deaths led to his parents' life of poverty and despair, which had driven Jasper's life like a ship in a storm.

"Even so, Jasper's childhood doesn't excuse his malevolence." Peter met his daughter's eyes. "I must protect Bella from him."

Aerowyn reached over and took hold of Peter's hand. "That, too, is in process. Gerard and I are repairing another story that will ultimately lead to Bella's happily-ever-after. I believe it will collide with Jasper's tale and give the pirate his second chance while assuring hers."

Peter finished his tea and studied his daughter's face. She had been his main emissary in reversing his wrongs, but at the moment, all his primary thought was how she so resembled her mother. Isla had been more like him.

The double loss pinched at his heart.

"You can't be in two places at once, my dear."

Gerard sat up and rested his huge head on Aerowyn's knee.

"In order for Bella to have her happy ending, I must work on another part of the story. You protected her from pirates and the creatures of Ageless Isle. Now it is time for you to stay home. Let me finish what I started."

Time crept by.

Peter poured cold tea into his cup but didn't drink it.

Aerowyn and Gerard waited.

"Very well. I trust you, my daughter," Peter finally said. "My time with the girl will end."

She stood, crossed to his chair, and hugged him.

His heart swelled. Aerowyn was noble and true, but the thought was bittersweet. Wendy would never see this side of their daughter. Another of his mistakes. He learned of Ageless Isle's ability to make humans immortal too late.

"Just a while longer, Father."

He nodded and managed a chuckle. "I've lived for hundreds of years, Aerowyn. I know that these things take time and patience. Our human guests might not agree, but I know you've been manipulating the puzzle pieces for years the same way I have been. They will come together at the perfect time."

She set a hand on Gerard's head. "Antoine's curse took a year to return the beast back to a man, but it would've been longer if Gerard didn't sacrifice himself—his humanity—out of love for his brother. Redemption is still unfolding. Jasper's blueprint for repair has been in the works for many years." She magicked the tea things away and drew a deep breath. "I must go, Father. I have work to do."

When she left, Peter sat alone in the dark.

In a mortal's timeline, the villains' path to redemption was excruciatingly long, but in the world of fairy tales, it was working out just as it needed to.

At least, that is what he hoped.

Chapter 30

Jasper

If Jasper had thought his experience with the redcaps had only been a nightmare, evidence proved otherwise: their blood was splattered all over the cage—a pungent reminder of his situation. There was no longer any doubt about Ageless Isle's magic and the boys' abilities.

He fidgeted and squirmed the more he obsessed over the need to wash away the blood spray. Confinement made the tight space even less tolerable. He needed to stretch his legs, but his hook caught on the bars whenever he tried to find a comfortable position. If his imprisonment impeded his success with the leprechaun challenge, Jasper would call foul play. Today, his goal was survival, then escape from the horrendous place before it was too late. On edge after the redcaps' invasion, he shuddered.

What other creepy things hid in the corners of the forest?

Even a pirate's life with battles and hand-to-hand combat was safer than a realm where redcaps were real. If only he hadn't set foot on this cursed island.

Despite his motto, regrets had been piling up since Bella came into his life. Was that Peter and Aerowyn's plan all along? The enchantress had warned him to change his ways before she gave him the cursed hook, and Peter had seemed overly protective of Bella, almost as if he was on the *Black Fear* strictly for her sake. Maybe they were using Bella to force him into developing a conscience?

His prison wobbled, and Jasper yelped, then swallowed his panic.

It was only that the leprechauns were lowering his cage to free him.

"Do ye promise to behave yeself?" Barney asked.

Jasper dipped his head slightly. "I'll do my best."

"Cross your heart and hope to die?" The boy used his index finger to trace an X across his chest and then made the gesture of a hangman's noose around his throat.

Jasper sighed. "I promise."

"Do what I did," the boy insisted.

Jasper harrumphed and imitated the boy's hand motions, but the boy interrupted. "While saying the words."

Grumbling at the childishness of the demand, Jasper appeased the annoying little sprite and repeated, "I promise. Cross my heart and hope to die." He crossed his heart and pulled on an imaginary rope around his neck. "Satisfied?"

The boy grinned and nodded, and his black mop of curly hair bounced up and down. The cage hit the ground and vanished, and the boy nudged Jasper into the forest where all the pirates, leprechauns, and Bella had assembled.

Jericho studied Jasper. "Now that you're here, we'll go back to Treasure Lagoon to begin your tests."

They headed toward the waterfalls, and sound of water grew louder the closer they came.

When they reached the lagoon, Jasper's mood soured even more. No mermaids sunbathed upon the rock. If this proved his downfall... Well. He'd wanted to see Cerise again.

"Men!" Jericho leaped on top of a stump. "We gather today to see if you are worthy enough to stay on Ageless Isle."

Jasper cleared his throat. "Are you going to explain the test or talk us to death?"

"Mind your manners, captain. After that outburst, you'll do the last trial, which won't be the same for any of you." Jericho met each man's gaze. "Your job is to retrieve one of each color of the precious gems from the waterfall and bring them to me. You can use any method, but beware that your greatest fears will be used against you."

"Wha' ye mean?" Jeb's voice shook.

"The water of Treasure Lagoon is full of mermaid foam."

Several pirates tilted their heads, and Jeb furrowed his brows.

"When mermaids die," Jericho explained, "they turn into sea foam, and most of their foam ends up here."

One young pirate gasped. "Ye mean, the water's full o' dead mermaids?"

The leprechaun boy scowled, pointed at the waterfall, and continued as if the pirate hadn't interrupted. "Their scales transform into the jewels you see there, but they also help the water see your deepest thoughts. It will use your fears against you to prevent you from taking the stones." Jericho made eye contact with every man, Jasper last of all. "You must conquer your fear to pass the test and live."

Jasper's hook quaked so he held it with his right hand. He'd run from his fears when he escaped his parents. Had faced them again the night before. He didn't want to be reminded of them ever again. They were the anchor that could sink him to the bottom of a sea of emotions where he'd drown.

"It's human nature to mask anxieties with hateful and selfish acts. We believe that if you can face your fears, you'll grow. And if you grow, you're less likely to mistreat others." Jericho glared at Jasper through narrowed eyes. "Of course, with you, it may only be you were born evil. Also, we don't want to share an island with humans who only wish to take from us."

Jasper fisted his on hand.

"I'd contribute by teaching you all to be—"

"Stop interrupting, Captain Falcon!" The leprechaun-boy pulled a large sword out of nowhere, and Jasper froze. "Or we'll kill you now!"

Everyone stared open-mouthed at the leprechaun's leader. He looked fierce enough to fulfill his promise.

Bella stared at the sword. Her hands shook slightly when she held them toward the boy. "Please, Jericho, finish what you were saying."

"As I was saying before the rude interruption," Jericho said through gritted teeth, "most humans don't choose to live here when they know the rules, even after they conquer their fears. They leave everything behind to get away as fast as they can, but the tests filter out the riff-raff and keep our existence safe and unscathed by greedy people." He scowled at Jasper. "King Peter, who gifted us with defensive magic, designed the test himself. He knew about the mermaid's lagoon and how it would weed out anyone who wanted to harm others and our world."

Bella frowned. "But you said before that some of the younglings come here from our world. Do the boys always succeed?" Her frown deepened into a scowl. "Or do you kill some of them?"

"Lost boys who can't pass the exam are sent back to their world. They usually live normal lives with humans. We aren't murderers like the captain." Jericho eyed Jasper.

"You could have fooled me." Jasper pointed. "Not only have you threatened to kill us multiple times, but two of your boys made minced meat out of those redcaps last night."

Bella gasped.

"Self-defense isn't murder, and neither is protecting someone under our care." Jericho raised his chin. "The ones who don't pass the trial leave. The redcaps, though, had already agreed to not harm anyone at our camp, and those two broke our pact. They picked death."

Jasper huffed and then rubbed his hook. "I concede. I appreciate the boys' interception on my behalf. And..." He paused to avoid a verbal misstep. "I understand the need to enforce rules and that being stern but fair always yields better results than being cruel. But, I protest, too. I was brought here under false pretenses, which has forced me to question everything before accepting it as fact."

Jericho narrowed his eyes at Jasper, then pulled a purple bag out of nowhere. "Each of you will draw a stone from the bag. Each flattened rock is numbered. Jasper won't participate in the lottery since he's going last."

One by one, the crew drew stones. Jeb's was clearly painted with the number one. He stepped forward, and sweat beaded his forehead. His jaw tightened.

"You'll retrieve one of each, diamond, sapphire, ruby, and emerald from the falls." Jericho repeated. "There are no rules on how you get them or how long it takes to bring them to me. Understand?"

Jeb nodded and followed a path around the lake then plunged in. As soon as he hit the water, a painful scream echoed from its depths. There was nothing to do but wait. There must have been magic involved because a human couldn't breathe under water for that long.

An hour later, Jeb swam to the shore and crept out, shaking. He had managed to bring back the jewels. His face was grim, and he was quiet but uninjured.

The day wore on. One by one each of Jasper's men jumped in. Every time, they screamed or shouted. Five sailors took only ten minutes, and six pirates were gone for about an hour. Only two failed to bring back any stones, but Jasper planned on leaving the island as soon as possible, so they would be safe with him.

He noticed the frightened determination of those who had succeeded. Something told him that each somehow emerged stronger and the experience hadn't broken any of them. Jasper was relieved because he needed his remaining crew to man the ship. It would have to be a smaller sloop with only one mast, but Jasper wouldn't worry about that now.

When his turn finally arrived, the sun had lowered, and visibility was poor. Jasper entered the water without hesitation. He wasn't going to allow this experience to break him, either.

Nothing happened. There was no reason to scream, and a surge of confidence gave him extra power as he kicked deeper into the lagoon. Several minutes passed before an unfamiliar yet beautiful mermaid swam up to him. She might have been friendly and alluring, but she was no Cerise. He tried to pass her, but she grabbed his arm.

The siren kissed him, and his mind gave into the sensation before he realized that he couldn't break free. His body was under her control as she began to siphon out all his memories.

Images moved quickly through his mind.

His mother. His father. The shabby shack of his childhood.

He watched the small boy—himself—cowering in the corner while his father screamed. Jasper's mother yanked the boy to his feet and slapped him. Jasper's skin stung.

His hand rose to his cheek, even though it was only a memory. Jasper knew this story.

He'd already escaped. He'd found a new life. He was strong and could easily protect the boy from those evil people. Was that what he was supposed to do to pass this test?

His father lifted a hand to slap small Jasper.

Jasper the man, stood tall and stared his father in the eye. He wasn't—wouldn't be—that frightened weakling any longer, but before the impact of the hand made contact, Jasper became his father. After the first punch, Jasper felt the crunch in his fist and pain in his jaw as if he had hurt himself.

These weren't fears. These were reminders of every agony he had inflicted, but all satisfaction was beaten out of him. Regret, remorse, terror...

The punishment was his own making.

In a sickening lurch, he was back in the lake. The mermaid had stopped kissing him, but she held him under, and he was suffocating as water filled his lungs.

No! I don't want to die in the water. I want to live in it.

The thought gave him the strength to fight, but when he resisted, the beautiful mermaid changed. Her smile grew vicious, and her teeth elongated into long, pointed razors. Her elegant cerulean tail turned a slimy, yellow green, then shifted to one shaped like an eel's. She lunged. Her sharp teeth went for his jugular, but he ducked. Jasper wriggled out of her grasp and swam as fast as he could. The eel-woman's muscular body was faster.

His muscles and lungs burned.

Blazing red hair swirled in front of him.

Cerise frantically pulled Jasper away.

When the eel-woman's chartreuse-colored body slithered closer, Cerise moved quicker. The witch's fingers grazed his foot, but Cerise lifted Jasper out of the water. He lay coughing on the rocks while she shot out of the lake after him, and her legs took shape. Her long, wavy hair covered everything except above her knees.

"If you don't get off Ageless Isle, you will die," she warned him. "I watched the other tests. Yours wasn't the same. I don't know what is going on here, but you're not safe." She took his hand and upended a fistful of jewels onto his palm. "Here, take these."

Jasper gulped in air. "Why are you helping me?"

"Aerowyn told me to." Cerise's eyes darted past him and back. "She didn't want you to die in Jericho's trial. You will be tested again, but it will be to redeem you from any regrets."

"But—"

Cerise covered his mouth with her hand. "I need to leave before anyone knows I'm here."

Then she pulled his head toward her and pressed her lips against Jasper's in a kiss that had him reeling from head to toe. Just as suddenly, she broke off and leapt back into the water. Her fin returned almost at once, and he watched her vanish into the depths.

The warmth of her lips lingered, but rather than sit there like a love-struck fool, Jasper stood. He needed to act.

The silvery moon glowed in the blackened sky, and Jasper followed the path behind the falls that led to the lagoon. Even from where he stood, he could see the fire and men drying off. Their conversation told Jasper that most of the pirates had gone back to the usual banter, as if their trial had simply been shore-leave.

Water-logged and tired, he carefully made his way down the slippery, narrow path. When he reached the clearing, worry was sketched on Bella's face. She really didn't deserve his treatment of her. It wasn't only because Cerise had criticized what he had done to Bella, but after he saw that his behavior mirrored Captain Starr's and his parents', Jasper was forced to face hard truths about himself.

He had become the thing he hated.

He couldn't let anyone know how Cerise helped him, so he squared his shoulders and put on a cocky smile. "Oy, mates. Your captain is alive and passed."

They all turned and faced him. Jericho looked disappointed, but relief washed over Bella and Jeb's expressions.

Jasper shoved the jewels into Jericho's palm. "Here are your blimey gems."

Jericho threw the stones into a pouch and sighed loudly. "Well, that's a bit disappointing. I had hoped to kill me a pirate today. Those who passed our exam may stay on the island."

Panic washed over the faces of the two pirates who failed, but Jasper quickly calmed their fears.

He met Jericho's eyes. "I don't wish to stay any longer and I'll take my men with me. I want to leave. How can I get a ship?"

"Really?" Peter popped out of nowhere as he spoke, making everyone jump. "You don't want to plunder all our treasures before you leave?"

"Peter, where have you been?" Bella asked, but she sounded tired.

"I watched from home to see your captain's fate."

Jasper held his peace, for once. Peter's smile reminded Jasper of Captain Starr's after he had killed someone.

"He's not my captain." Bella jutted out her chin. "But, if he'll take me home to New Orleans, I will call him by that title."

He bowed slightly. "King Peter, you said you can get us a ship. I would be grateful for your assistance."

The fae king lifted one eyebrow. "You've seemed to have a change in manners."

"Those tests gave me a lot to evaluate about my life choices." Jasper said. Just because he faced his past didn't mean he needed to tell that manipulative fae the details. "Can you get us a ship?"

His crew crowded behind him and Jasper heard several muttered, "Yes, we want to leave."

The two who failed their test spoke clearly. "We support that decision."

Peter nodded. "Stay with the leprechauns tonight and then travel to shore during the day. The dangers you faced when you were caged last night will still be out there, as will those you didn't see."

Jasper grunted. "How'd I manage to forget about the island's deadly creatures?" He rubbed his chin. "Yes, I agree we should sleep in the leprechauns' camp first."

A smug smile crossed the king's face. "You've definitely grown wiser since you first arrived on this isle."

Jericho stood by Peter. "Since you're staying another night and passed the trial, you may have a bed tonight. Tomorrow, we'll help you set sail." His cheeks lifted in a grin. "The leprechauns are glad you're not going to stay."

The humans and leprechauns filed back to the encampment in silence. Even Bella didn't prattle, which left Jasper plenty of time to think. At dinner, Jasper summoned up a delicious stew that filled him satisfactorily, but his thoughts kept wandering back to Cerise. She had saved his life, even though he was little more than a stranger. His whole life, he was either feared or used. Had anyone ever looked at him as having value?

After dinner, the leprechauns led the pirates back to their treehouses, and Jasper gladly accepted a small hut of his own.

If he were to dream, he hoped it would be of the red-headed mermaid who took up much of his mind and heart.

Chapter 31

Bellarose

A fter the men and boys dispersed, Peter lingered at the dining table.

"King Peter?" Bella set her water cup aside and turned in her chair to face him. "You've said you wanted me to be safe."

He inclined his head in agreement.

She crossed her arms. "So why didn't you whisk me back to New Orleans? Why did you allow Jasper to kidnap me if you were so worried about my well-being?"

"My motives will have to remain unknown to you at this time." His eyes darted and changed colors.

"But I promise you none of that was done for evil purposes."

"Even the great fae king couldn't predict all the dangers this journey had to offer." Bella pushed her chair away from the now empty table. She didn't trust him.

"Cerise said a sea witch caused that typhoon. What if she had managed to drown me?"

"I was briefly concerned about that storm." The king stopped and glared into the trees. "I had not foreseen the sinking of the *Black Fear*. I would have unveiled my disguise and rescued you before you drowned, but Cerise beat me to it." He rubbed his pendant. "I don't know her personally, but she really is kinder to humans than most mermaids are."

"So, you admit that you're planning something," she said as she paced. "If your plans involve me, why can't I know what they are?"

Peter motioned for Bella to sit, but she refused. He shook his head. "They involve several people, but for my intentions to succeed, you cannot know. If you change your actions because of something I tell you, the plans could be misdirected to another fate."

The more Bella thought about Peter manipulating her life without telling her why, the more frustrated she became. She wrung her hands to keep them busy when she really wanted to hit something with her fists.

"My whole life is a series of events I have no control over," she snapped. "I've been patiently giving you the benefit of the doubt, but it's getting exhausting."

Peter pursed his lips.

"I'm not a pawn on a chessboard." She stopped. Maybe she was only a pawn. Her stomach tightened. What if...

Was her family's disastrous move to America part of Peter's scheme?

Bella rubbed her temples.

She would never have met Gerard, never been exposed to his rude, sometimes inappropriate behavior.

Bella resumed her pacing.

Yes, Gerard had transformed, and yes, she gained Brooke as a friend, but what good was that when Jasper ended up kidnapping her? The one person that made New Orleans enjoyable was Quinn, and now even her friendship with him was ruined.

She spun to face Peter.

"You," she whispered. "You made this happen."

Peter mumbled words in a strange language.

Her eyelids closed, and her body slacked. Before she finished questioning Peter, she blacked out.

Bella opened her eyes. A large library? Not a forest? Was she dreaming? The pumpkin tabby curled up on her lap and purring loudly seemed real enough. She absentmindedly brushed her hand over his soft fur as she absorbed her surroundings. She should have been in a panic, yet the sweet feline—his tag said his name was Hobbes—calmed her nerves.

The tantalizing scents of pine, cinnamon, and baked goods wafted through the air. Was this part of Ageless Isle? Was Jericho testing her even though he said he already had and that she'd passed?

She lifted the sweet cat off her lap and put him on the cozy chair to continue his nap, but her clothes felt wrong. When had she changed into men's britches? No, wait. She knew this. These were... jeans. From a modern world.

The spectacular library baffled Bella. Shelves of books filled the walls, and a warm fire crackled next to the comfortable lounge chair where the cat now rested. It had to be a fantasy world.

"We're not in Kansas anymore," she heard herself say, but the longer she focused on the room, the more she recalled that this *was* Gastonville, Colorado—the place she belonged to.

"It's just like Dorothy, the character in a book, belonged in Kansas, not in Oz," she said. "Ageless Isle is my Oz."

She plopped down on an overstuffed chair. *Peter Pan, Beauty and the Beast, The Little Mermaid...* Had she been inside those stories? But her life wherever, or whenever it was had been so real. It couldn't be.

The fire's flickering was spellbinding.

Her eyelids drooped...

· ▪ ● ⚘ ● ▪ ·

"Bella, did you hear me?"

She startled at the voice as well as the hand on her shoulder. "I'm sorry. I must have fallen asleep. What did you say?"

King Peter peered at her with concern on his face. "I said tomorrow is a long day, and you should get some sleep." He patted her on the arm. "Were you dreaming?"

"A bit, but it's all gone now. Just a feeling of comfort, but it was confusing."

He chuckled. "Confusing comfort? You must be tired if you dream right away."

Bella rubbed her eyes and stood. *But wasn't she standing before she dreamed?* "I ought to say thank you."

"For?"

"You kept me safe from Jasper, storms, and the dangers of Ageless Isle."

Drowsiness made her sway, and she held onto Peter to keep from falling. Hadn't he said something about how she wasn't supposed to be on the *Black Fear*, and that his real motivation for his disguise as Sven was to stop Jasper from finding Ageless Isle, but he had done his best to help her as well? It seemed a little foggy in her memory.

"Bella, you're going to fall asleep standing up. Go to bed so you'll have energy for tomorrow's trip back to the ocean."

She yawned. "Yes, this adventure has worn me out."

"Will you be able to climb up the ladder to your bed?"

Bella tried to stifle a second yawn, then gave into it. "Yes, I can manage."

While she gingerly climbed the ladder to Jericho's cabin, the boy appeared suddenly to help steady her.

She slurred, "You d-o-on't need to help. I fine."

"You can barely stand straight."

"I fine."

After she had crawled into bed, he went outside and closed the door behind him.

She heard him call out, "She's safe, Your Majesty. Good night!"

Bella wanted to say good night to Peter as well, but she was too tired. The next thing she knew, she fell into a dreamless sleep.

Chapter 32

Peter

The incantation Peter had cast over Bella should be enough to erase her suspicions. At least, he hoped it would. Unraveling the truth of the fairy tales and her real life would ruin her happily ever after. She had to continue to believe that she was Bella, a young aristocrat who had journeyed from France to America and lost her parents on the way. The lore she had read in her real world must be fixed.

Once Jericho shouted that she was safely ensconced in the hut, the king transported instantly to his own home in the woods. He sat on the plush chair in his den and flipped through a primitive photo album. Though it was such a simple thing, Peter enjoyed perusing through the pages that he had spelled so that the people moved within the picture.

Wendy blew him kisses from the page as if she were still alive. He kissed the air back as if she would ever know.

Aerowyn's voice broke into the silence, and he startled. "Father, what are you looking at?"

He snapped the album shut and turned to find his daughter and that wolf in the doorway. "Photos of your mother. What are you doing here?"

Gerard sniffed the air.

I wonder what he smells.

"I thought I'd check up on your progress." She grabbed the photobook from his lap and opened it up to the page he had just been on. "Was Mother's death the catalyst?"

Peter scrunched his brows. "Catalyst for what?"

"After Mother died, you withdrew, disappeared. When you returned you had new rules." Aerowyn sat down, and Gerard settled on his haunches next to her. "First you said we couldn't go beyond the dark forest, and then we began cursing people who were selfish."

Peter sighed. "You skipped the part about your sister, Isla."

Aerowyn turned to a photo of her sister. "I know. I didn't want to bring up painful memories."

"Well, you did."

"Doing so was not my intent."

"I know," he said again. He had known, down deep, that Isla was wild. He should have guessed she would grow bored and travel to the human realm where she faced dragon fire.

That, too, was Peter's fault. He had created the beast in the first place, and Aerowyn could never know.

"I shouldn't have punished Callista by turning her into a hideous sea snake." He stood and grabbed another album off the shelf. He paged through to find a photo of Isla when she was a child. "A mere mermaid couldn't have stopped Isla. Someday I want to give Callista her chance at redemption as you want for Jasper." He touched Isla's cheek in the picture and the magicked image reacted as if real. "I was impulsive and angry from grief."

Aerowyn reached over and touched his hand. "I was angry, too, but I needed you, and you disappeared."

"Yes, because I was going to fix all the wrongs in the universe, but in the process, I upturned worlds and changed the path of all fairy tales." He tapped his fingers on the book. "Callista and other villains were the result, and now I won't be able to repair anything without Bella's help."

"I never understood how Bella was going to fix anything," Aerowyn confessed.

Peter closed the photo album and put it back on the shelf. He looked out his den's window to avoid his daughter's judgmental eyes.

"Bella's gift of storytelling will reverse the damage done to the fairy tales and put them back to their original outcomes."

"Oh, Father." Moments passed, then Aerowyn asked, "How does Bella's imagination help reverse warped stories?"

"If she finishes this adventure with a happily-ever-after, I will take her story and put it into the ancient tome of tales. Then all the twisted stories will go back to their original plots."

"Father, look at me," Aerowyn demanded. "What proof do you have that will work?"

"Back in the Kingdom of Magic, I read some of the ancient manuscripts in our archives and they explained what needed to be done," Peter lied to his daughter.

He hadn't been back to the archives after he moved to Ageless Isle. The manuscripts told him how to create a dragon. He'd done it, but now he was done with them. He used his power to do whatever he wanted to forget his pain. He only wanted to fix the stories now, because he didn't want to admit to Aerowyn—the only one left who loved him—the details of what he had really done.

Aerowyn stared tight-lipped. She didn't seem convinced.

He changed the subject. "Did you know that Bella continues to remember the real life we pulled her from?"

"No, but I haven't been around her as much as you."

"I had to put a memory spell on her. Bella, like other humans, needs to continue to believe that fairy tales are fiction."

"Yes, I agree." Aerowyn stood and Gerard followed. "I'm going to get ready to set in motion my plan for Jasper. Once he's at sea again, he'll be given his second chance."

Peter nodded. "I will have to go back to the beach to craft them a new ship since Callista ruined the original one."

Aerowyn disappeared in a mist without a goodbye or hug. The king sat down and leaned forward to rest his palm against his face. That was how she had treated him ever since Peter manipulated her to help him rid the world of selfishness. He missed that, too.

If he didn't reverse the issues his anger and pain produced in the first place, fantasy would run amok beyond the pages of each tome. He couldn't predict everything, but if the damage his dragons had caused was any indication, he didn't have to look too hard for the answer.

Libraries would no longer be a portal for people to enter stories.

They would become a door for mythical creatures to enter the human realm.

Chapter 33

Jasper

The odor of coffee and bacon alerted Jasper to the fact others were awake. He lumbered down the ladder of his treehouse. His brows furrowed when he saw his men scooping air out of empty bowls and shoveling invisible food into their mouths. Why did he smell it if he couldn't see the food?

Jasper sighed and forced his imagination to invent something delicious. In mere moments, steam rose from the bacon, eggs, and fresh bread on his plate. He grimaced, though at the young man next to him, who had imagined gloppy porridge. That only made sense if that was the best food the lad had ever known.

Someone offered him a greeting, and Jeb quickly shushed him. Jasper smirked. Jeb evidently remembered Jasper didn't appreciate chatter first thing in the morning.

Bella arrived before he finished his first plateful. Her face was puffy, and her hair was a mess.

"Good morning, Miss Bonnay. You look rather ragged today."

"I feel like you look after drinking all night." She rubbed her eyes.

Jasper grinned. "Did you finally give into the fun and partake in spirits?"

"Never." She glared at him but took a neighboring seat between him and Jeb, across from Jericho. "That doesn't even sound fun. Anyway, I didn't feel any different until bedtime. It was like someone drugged me. I was exhausted, but sleep should have fixed that problem."

The curly-headed boy—Barney?—next to Jericho jumped to his feet. Jericho, too, stood, and the breakfast noise fell away.

The boys' leader put his hands on his hips, surveyed the hushed table, and demanded, "Did any of you spike Bella's drink last night?"

The leprechauns shook their heads, and the pirates only returned blank stares.

Bella frowned at Jasper. "I'm sure it was just over-exertion. I probably won't ever feel completely rested until I'm in a place I consider home."

Jasper drummed his fingers on the table. Hadn't Peter and Bella stayed behind last night while everyone else went to bed? Sven had been the herb master. A scowl pulled Jasper's face down. Peter, the scoundrel, had probably done it, but announcing his suspicions wouldn't do Jasper or Bella any good.

As if Jasper's thoughts had summoned him, Peter appeared out of nowhere. "How is everyone doing?"

Bella rubbed her temples. "I have a bit of a headache, but I think we're ready to leave the island."

Jericho slapped his hands together. "It's time to return to the cliffs. If we don't leave soon, it will be dark before we reach them." He turned to Jasper and clarified, "We don't have any arrangements with the redcaps or the jackaroons past our camp border."

"What are jackaroons?" Bella asked.

Jasper took another swig of rum to hide a flash of fear. The redcaps were bad enough.

The leprechaun shuddered. "Believe me, you don't want to know."

"Getting down those cliffs will be hard," Bella said. "Unless Tilly is willing to help us? Or do we have to climb down?"

Jericho's eyes wrinkled in the corners. "I don't think you are strong enough to climb the cliffs. By the looks of your group, no one here—not even the strapping Captain Falcon—could manage it." He smirked. "Especially with only one hand."

Jasper ignored the comment about his missing hand and instead flexed a bicep. "Strapping? Why, thank you for noticing."

Bella rolled her eyes, but he expected that.

He hid a more genuine smile. His boasting had served it purpose if her mood lightened and she asked no more questions about jackaroons or the like.

"Shall we?" he asked with a deep bow.

Bella huffed. If she hadn't looked so miserable, he would've said she jaunted after the leprechaun leader.

Jasper grinned, and the need to impress the others shrank, somehow leaving him feeling... taller.

Unlike the journey to the leprechaun's camp, the pirates remained unbound and walked side-by-side. They chatted freely but kept their cursing and unseemly jokes to a whisper to avoid Peter's ire. Obviously, memories of the previous day's test had faded until they approached the lake again.

As they passed the water, the only noises were feet breaking twigs or padding over moss covered paths. The mood flipped to sober quicker than that storm had crushed the *Black Fear*. Was each pirate reliving their test? Jasper was as he, too, kept an eye on the sparkling blue water. Cerise had warned him to leave the island. Perhaps, once he decided to do just that, his life was no longer at risk, but he kept his guard up just in case the leprechauns or Peter wanted to double cross him. After all, her warning didn't tell him where the threat would come from. The fae themselves could be the danger, not just strange animals or whatever else here.

The group remained quiet even after the lake was no longer in sight. Their silence ate Jasper. He had to think of something that would help.

Then, he knew a way to improve morale and gain information on the slippery fae who had been Sven.

Jasper jogged to the front of the line and caught with Bella. "Would you be willing to tell me another story to pass the time?"

Bella narrowed her eyes. "Really? You want me to tell you a tale?"

"Yes, it's better than this deafening silence." He then said quietly, "I think seeing the lake again dredged up some bad things. Perhaps it would help distract them?"

She glanced over her shoulders at the solemn men, then sighed. "I don't have a bunch of anecdotes memorized, but I suppose I could improvise the parts I don't exactly remember. What type would you prefer?" She added hopefully, "Maybe a romance?"

Jasper coughed. What did she think he was? "I can handle a romance, if it has action too." He paused for effect. "Do you know any stories about immortals?"

She turned her head to stare at him. "Yes, but you knew that."

"So, the leprechauns in your story were immortal? Because I didn't know, only assumed."

"No, it wasn't that one." Bella looked around, then leaned closer. "You know, *The Scorned Fae*, the story about Peter's daughter."

"Oh," Jasper said as innocently as he could. "I forgot about that one. Couldn't you share it but change the names and some details? To keep from bringing up the king's painful past."

She bit her lip. "I doubt I could alter it enough to make it unrecognizable to him. I'll think of a different legend."

Jasper wasn't ready to give up. With the correct questions, he knew Bella would share the information. From what he remembered, Peter's daughter was immortal—and then she wasn't.

What caused her to die?

And could he use that to protect himself against Peter if he attempted to kill Jasper.

From the front of the party, the fae king half-turned and met Jasper's eyes. Bah. He'd forgotten the fae could evidently read minds. Jasper brought his thoughts and imagination around to summon a fresh apple. When it appeared, he focused all his mental energy on the crisp taste and the juice rolling down his chin.

He wasn't going to risk his chances to getting off this island and returning to the sea—to Cerise. That was exactly the life for him.

Chapter 34

Bellarose

Bella's legs and feet hurt. She had worked hard back at the de la Rose plantation, but two days of walking after surviving a shipwreck was entirely different. Sweat dripped down the back of her neck. The last thing she wanted to do was talk when her legs ached with each step and she was nearly out of breath.

Jasper had fallen silent, so she studied him from the corner of her vision. At least he no longer undressed her with his eyes, for which she was thankful. Threats from Peter and Jericho might have been what was keeping Jasper in check, but the pirate was as sly as a fox. Maybe he was scheming about what to do with her once they obtained a new ship. She would feel safer if Peter joined them on the trip back to New Orleans, but she had the feeling he wouldn't.

Her plans to escape when she got onto the island died out once she realized Sven was a powerful fae king and had wanted her on whatever journey this was. Even if she ran away from the group, her chances of survival with the dangerous creatures on Ageless Isle were worse than staying with Jasper.

With her attention on the tall man beside her instead of the ground before her, Bella tripped over a tree root. Jasper effortlessly kept her from falling with his un-hooked hand, but even though he hadn't leered at her since the ship, she pulled away as soon as she was steady on her feet. It wouldn't do to encourage the man in any way.

Finally, she decided. "I could tell you a yarn I remember about a cliff similar to the one we're heading to."

Jasper looked disappointed but gestured for her to continue.

"There once was a girl who lost her true love, when he was kidnapped by pirates."

Jasper's far-off gaze confirmed her suspicion that he wasn't really listening to her story, but that didn't stop her. She used voices for each character, and several of the pirates and the leprechauns slowed to walk close so they could listen.

Barney, the boy who talked about imagination asked, "Did her true love die?"

"You have to wait to find out." Bella grinned. "I'm not to that part yet."

Jeb asked her to repeat a part he'd missed.

The journey went by quickly as the heroine was abducted by strangers, then rescued by a masked man. Bella's voice cracked from overuse, and Jericho handed her a jug of water. She continued to the end of the tale, and the telling of it gave her courage. True love could conquer death. Eventually the girl was reunited with her true love, and they lived happily ever after.

Bella's happy ending would be Quinn. The hope of reuniting with him one day gave her strength to continue walking. After she returned to New Orleans, she would decide on how to approach Quinn, but that didn't need to be decided today.

Chapter 35

Jasper

J asper listened to Bella's tale with only half his attention. Men and boys gravitated to her. Barney asked a lot of questions. Jasper clapped with moderate enthusiasm when she finally finished, but what drew him back into the present was the sound of waves. It was medicine for his soul. Whenever his past miseries haunted him, the soothing scents and vibrations of the ocean brought him peace.

Perhaps it had always been tied in with Cerise and how she had rescued him. He had been obsessed with treasure and replenishing what was lost at sea when the *Black Fear* sank, but those things wouldn't satisfy the hollow ache in his heart. He knew that now—not that he could reveal that to anyone when he was a pirate captain.

Instead, he only said, "What? Are we already here?"

"Oh," Bella exclaimed as they stopped on top of the cliffs. "It looks like a painting. As if the ocean is touching the stars."

It did seem like the blackened sky and sparkling stars were connected. Jasper closed his eyes for a moment and breathed in the briny air. It was like coming home.

Then, he turned to Peter. "Are we going to have to spend the night on shore again? I believe you could magic us a ship, if you were inclined, though we do have to get down there first."

"Will we use that dust from your fairy friend, King Peter?" Bella asked.

"Yes," Peter said. "Unless Captain Falcon wants to try climbing down to prove he's as strong as the pirate in your story."

Jasper ignored the jab at his ego and gave the fae a half-smile. "That was only a story, and no, I don't need to prove I'm strong by being careless."

Peter called out for Tilly, who appeared at once. This time she didn't ask what the king wanted. Throwing a poisonous glare Jasper's way, she sprinkled pixie dust over each person and flew away without saying a word.

"You recall that this only works with happy thoughts," Peter reminded them. "Leprechauns, stay at the top of the cliffs in case any of the humans need rescuing."

The boys gave the king snappy salutes, then lined up to say goodbye to Bella. The girl shook hands with Jericho and the boys, then paused in front of Barney. The lad had cozied up to her two nights ago when she told the story about the leprechauns and again during the long walk to the shore.

For the first time, Jasper saw deeper than the surface. Barney was the essence of innocence. He smiled at the boy who Jasper might have been if his parents hadn't been brutal drunkards.

She gave the boy a hug. "Don't ever stop imagining fantastic things."

He blushed. "I won't."

Bella and the pirates rose into the air, then descended smoothly to the beach, but Jasper stood alone with the leprechauns. None of his racing thoughts—having a new ship, having treasure, sailing back to New Orleans—were good enough to get him off the ground. The group was half-way down the cliff before Jasper allowed himself to think of the impossibility of finding Cerise and joining her in the ocean. His feet left the clifftops, but dropped when he reminded himself it was only fantasy. Then, the memory of Cerise's sincere eyes and that kiss in the lagoon drove off the practical and gave him flight. He landed on the sandy beach right after everyone else.

Peter noticed he was last—of course he did—and looked him up and down. "I suppose being a brutal pirate makes it difficult to conjure up happy thoughts."

"Happiness isn't necessary to give me satisfaction." Jasper huffed. "Although that is not your business."

"I wasn't prying," the king said calmly. "I was observing."

The fae's arrogance drove Cerise's image out of Jasper's head. He clenched his fist and then forced his hand flat against his leg. The temptation to punch the smug king in his pretty face wouldn't bode well for him. His best bet for escaping was to return to the seas and forget he had ever seen Ageless Isle or met Peter.

Besides, Peter probably spies on my thoughts and already knows the truth.

Jasper squared his shoulders. "Stop making observations and tell me how I can obtain a ship."

Bella and the pirates gaped.

Peter's eyes turned violet again. "You can get your ship back—or a different one—with a strong imagination. The problem is that you have only twelve men counting yourself, so you may need a smaller vessel. The magic on this island will produce a ship as real as any you could steal, but it won't yield sailors." Peter pointed to the ocean. "You can take whatever you conjure up back to New Orleans, where you will return Bella to her friends."

"Does Bella want to return to Louisiana or stay with me?" Jasper flashed a smile that had Peter's eyes turn a brighter violet. Then, Jasper shrugged. "All teasing aside and though the moonlit night highlights your beauty, Miss Bonnay, I no longer want to court you."

She gasped. "You don't?"

The relief on her face almost made him laugh. Instead, Jasper bowed deeply and winked at her. "I have great admiration for you, but alas, your heart seems to belong to someone else."

Bella's face reddened as she realized what Jasper implied. Quinn had her heart and now she knew that Jasper was aware of it.

"I'm glad you changed your mind, Captain Falcon. I didn't feel like I belonged to Rose Manor, but it seems that I prefer safety of land over sea." She bit her lip. "Although, will they think I'm horrible after the letters you forced me to write?"

The letters... He'd asked Sven-who-was-really-Peter to deliver those and kill Quinn. A lump of regret formed in his gut, but he quickly dismissed it. Bah. Had he done as he was told? Jasper glanced at the king, then cleared his throat. "I'm sure you can explain to them that I forced you to write those."

"The voyage is long; the sea witch, Callista, is still out there; but my job here is complete," Peter stated. Discuss what will happen *after* you set sail. Captain, you say you will not harm my dear friend, but if you do, I will find you. And I will curse you with more than a hooked hand."

Jasper glared at the fae. "I already said I won't pursue Bella. There's no need to threaten me like a child."

Behind him, Jeb said, "Cap'n tells the truf. He kept us safe from Cap'n Starr as promised."

One of the other pirates stepped forward. "Never cheats us, neither."

The men's confidence bolstered his spirit. Jasper didn't need to control Bella to maintain their respect.

He raised his chin in defiance of the fae king's accusation. "My word is final."

Chapter 36

Peter

The humans needed a ship, even though sailing put them back in Callista's domain. She had put a wrench in Peter's original plan, which made their journey more perilous. And before her tale could be mended, Jasper needed to be dealt with.

So. A ship. That required another lie, but an easy enough one.

Peter began, "To create something similar to the *Black Fear*, I think you all need to wish for the same thing." He waited while the pirates thought. Some took longer than others, but Peter remained patient. "The ship can have different elements of what each of you want, but you will all have to agree on whatever it is."

Bella's mind was whirling with anxiety and dread. "Are you going with us?"

"No, my mission is complete," he repeated. When two lines formed between Bella's eyebrows, he added gently, "Don't worry, you will be safe. I have ways to protect you even when I'm not on board."

"Then why did you join this crew and pretend to be Sven?"

He smiled. Although, Bella's curiosity knew no end, it wasn't time for answers.

Peter folded his hands. "That explanation is for another time."

Even without reading her mind, Bella's frustration evident, but Jasper grinned from ear to ear. His thoughts of destroying Peter had vanished. Once Peter dug beyond Jasper's cluttered thoughts from his pirate life, Peter saw Jasper's deepest heart's desire. He reread the thought.

It was Jasper's true happiness, but only if he took the second chance Aerowyn was going to offer him.

Jeb's hesitant thoughts interrupted Peter. The ginger-haired pirate bowed awkwardly. "I wills miss ye Peter—I mean, Yur Majesty."

"It was a pleasure meeting you," Peter allowed himself to smile. "I trust you will keep Bella from harm."

Jeb saluted. "Yes, sir."

"Attention, you seadogs! No one is going anywhere without a ship." Jasper clapped his hands. "Men, start concentrating on the *Black Fear*. Remember all its nooks and crannies. I want an exact, if smaller, duplicate."

His men squeezed their eyes shut.

Jasper's baritone boomed over the sand. "Imagine our vessel into being, or whatever it is you call that mystical mumbo jumbo." He looked over at Bella.

"I will focus on a more improved *Black Fear* so Bella will have her own room and not have to use mine."

"Thank you," she murmured, but Bella's thoughts were less focused on the craft and more on the journey home. Peter hid an affectionate smile. If it had taken everyone present to create the new *Black Fear*, she wouldn't have contributed to it at all.

Of course, Peter had to craft a ship without their help. It would be able to mostly sail itself, so a bigger crew wasn't necessary. His confidence grew. With Aerowyn helping, with his plans in motion, nothing else would hinder his goals to repair the twisted fairy tales.

Chapter 37

Jasper

I t was one thing to imagine rum. Conjuring a ship was entirely different, but while Jasper focused on the things he wanted most in the *Black Fear II*, a faint outline, as blurry and transparent as a ghost ship appeared on the water. Gradually, the shape grew solid.

Jasper would have to enlist more men before he took on larger vessels, but this one would have what they needed to take them far from Ageless Isle. And that was all Jasper really cared about.

When the men saw the ship and cheered, Jasper held up his hand and hook to silence them.

"Rather than sleep on the beach tonight, let's go to our new home aboard *Black Fear II*."

"I'm not even tired," one of the crewmen volunteered.

"I can stay up and help in any way you need if it means returning to New Orleans earlier." Bella's earlier scowl vanished, replaced with an eager, hopeful expression.

"Good." Somehow, Jasper kept his jangling nerves from making his voice shake. Focus. Get off the island. "We will eventually need to take turns sleeping, but we leave tonight."

Peter studied him, and the fae's unnerving gaze made Jasper's skin crawl. When the king approached, however, he simply handed Jasper a glass container filled with sparkling sand.

"This is Tilly's pixie dust. One of the men will have to sprinkle it on the sails when you reach the open seas. It will help you avoid Callista the sea witch and take you to your world where you can navigate back to New Orleans."

Jasper eyed the sand with skepticism. Could he trust Peter's jar full of magical dust? And how would that small amount transport such a large ship away from Ageless Isle? Still, he wasn't going to stay, no matter how many doubts he had. He took the clear crock, which was heavier than he would have expected, and handed it to Bella.

The pirates untied the lifeboat they used after the storm and pulled it into the water to row to the *Black Fear II*.

Jasper asked, "Bella, do you mind getting wet or may I carry you?"

She eyed him and then the skiff. "I don't mind a little salt water. I've been through worse."

Bella hiked up her skirt and sloshed through the shallow water. Jeb lifted her into the small vessel, and then Jasper stepped into the water. Perhaps he should've said thanks to the king, but he merely turned and nodded before he left the shore.

Jasper hoisted himself into the skiff. He raised his hook and yelled. "Men, we set sail tonight!"

They cheered as they rowed to the leeward side where a rope ladder dangled from the top of the pristine ship. Eager to set sail, the pirates rushed up the cords. Bella was slower, but even she managed to reach the ship's deck without too much assistance. Jasper was last to come aboard the new *Black Fear II*.

"Ah!" Jasper inhaled loudly. "It feels good to be aboard a ship again." He pivoted toward the crew and commanded, "Into positions!"

Their cheers resounded, and every man found his place. They broke out into spontaneous song and laughter.

Jasper glanced back at Ageless Isle. Peter waved to them from the beach and then turned into mist. Jasper blinked, and the king was gone.

Good riddance.

He took in a huge breath of salt air. He would find his fortune the old-fashioned pirate way from now on instead of from places of immortality or exotic riches. He'd leave that folklore drivel to one of Bella's books.

Based on the men's joyful reactions, Jasper wasn't the only one relieved to get a lengthy distance from the disturbing island.

His spirits lifted and he sang along with the crew.

Yo ho, yo ho, me mate and I will find
Yo ho, yo ho, treasure beyond the sky.
Yo ho, yo ho, me mate and I will see
Yo ho, yo ho, how amazing it will be.

"Captain?"

He stopped singing and turned abruptly.

Bella gave him a sheepish smile. "I can't sleep. Is there anything I can do to help?"

He looked her up and down. "A week ago, I would have said stand where I can drink in your beauty, but I'm a changed man."

She set down the pixie dust and gave disdainful look. "I never thought your behavior was charming, if that's what you meant it to be."

"I suppose I thought it was since it won over many." He chuckled. "Anyway, for now, you can keep an eye out for sea witches."

She didn't move to watch the water, only glared.

"Can I *truly* trust that you've changed? Until Peter and Aerowyn intervened, you made inappropriate advances toward me."

"True, but now I have different priorities to preoccupy my mind."

Bella eyed him. "You know, I think Peter read our thoughts. I don't believe we conjured up anything with our ideas."

Even though the same suspicion had crossed his mind, Jasper raised an eyebrow. "I'm surprised at you. I thought you admired Peter, but you are implying he spied on our thoughts like a fiend?"

"Not exactly a fiend. It just seems strange to think that we created those tents on our first night. Or that everything else miraculous on the island from our own abilities." She grabbed the deck's rail. "He probably even manufactured this ship for us."

"I agree with you." Jasper said. "I also think he stopped the storm and saved as many of us as he could. He was especially interested in keeping you alive."

"Do you have anything to prove your theories?"

"I don't have solid proof, only conjecture, but there were too many things from my past that were used against me to be a product of magic alone." Jasper rubbed his hook. "While those who lived on the isle, like Tilly and the redcaps, probably had their own abilities. I suspect those leprechauns didn't have magic until Peter gifted it to them."

She huffed. "For once, I agree with you. They were immortal because of Ageless Isle, but their backstories came from human families and nothing out of the ordinary."

"Doesn't that make you question Peter's motives for bringing us to the island in the first place?"

"Yes," she confessed. "I suspect I have something to do with it, and he needed an excuse to spy on our fears and secret happinesses, if he didn't know them before."

The *Black Fear II* rose on a swell, and Jasper focused on the wheel—a trick he was only beginning to master with one hand and one hook. Bella's revelations had taken him by surprise, but Peter's warning about the sea witch echoed in Jasper's head. Of course, there was no way any of them could spot her or any other monster lurking in the ocean before it was too late, but Bella didn't have to know that.

Jasper checked the stars to make certain they were on course, then looked over at Bella. "Until you get tired, here's my spyglass." He pulled it out from his inside coat pocket. "I'm not sure you'll be able to see what's-her-name in the ocean, but you can try."

Bella accepted his spyglass. "Cerise and Peter called her Callista. My guess is that Peter knew more than he ever told us about that situation."

Jasper's heart hitched a little at the mention of Cerise, but then he forced his thoughts back to the present. No use dreaming about the impossible. Even if he could see her in the ocean, it wasn't what he truly wanted. At least he had the small hope.

"He did know more, but who knows? Maybe she'll leave us alone." He exhaled. "We'd be powerless if she decided to slash our ship apart again. We can't afford to lose any men. Hopefully, if we see her before the attack, we can prepare better."

Bella nodded solemnly. "I'll keep an eye out for her."

After several minutes of quiet, she released a shuddering yawn that made him yawn, too. Bella might have wanted to help, but Jasper suspected she'd fall asleep soon. Even as he thought it, her eyes closed, her head fell forward, and she jerked upright. She put the telescope to her eye and yawned again.

"I don't see anything. I think we're safe enough for now." With that, she handed him back the spyglass and staggered off to her room.

The smile that twitched across his face vanished when the breeze turned icy for a moment.

A sense of foreboding crept over Jasper. They were in a strange ocean where mythical creatures existed. Something—any-thing—could go wrong at any moment.

He scanned the ocean, but even though he saw nothing unusual, the prickling on the back of his neck didn't go away.

Chapter 38

Gerard

Footsteps snapped Gerard from his nap. He jerked his head up from his comfortable floor-cushion. His nostrils twitched as the floral aromas of Aerowyn's home were overpowered by a woodsy scent.

Peter.

Gerard tilted his head to see the fae king scowling down at him.

Gerard growled. *I don't like you either.*

Aerowyn patted Gerard on the head and spoke to him mentally, *It's only Father.*

So, I smell and see.

I asked him to come. She stroked his head gently. *I am safe. We are safe. You can go back to your nap.*

I'm not tired.

Her yellow dress swooshed past Gerard on her way to grab the kettle from the stove.

She motioned to the table. "Father, please sit down for some tea."

The fae king moved past Gerard.

I wonder what he wears under his white dress?

Aerowyn threw him a pleading look. *It's a tunic, not a dress. Gerard, please. You know he can pry into people's thoughts. Please be careful.*

He doesn't think I'm people.

Of course he does.

Peter sat down and sighed. "It's disconcerting to see a wild animal in your house."

Told you.

"He's not wild," Aerowyn said covering Gerard's growl at the insult. "But, Father, I need to state the obvious. The fairy tale characters are still not following their stories."

She poured steaming liquid into Peter's cup, and the familiar scents of lavender and honey filled the air. When she sat down. Gerard trotted over to sit at her side.

"I know, Aerowyn. We need you-know-who..." He eyed Gerard. "Does he have to be here?"

"Yes. I will not put him outside. He belongs here until his story plays out." Aerowyn brushed a hand over Gerard's neck and he melted into her touch.

"Fine." Peter took a long drink of tea. "We need her to have a happy ending before the tales are fixed."

Bella? She was the common link with all the people he and Aerowyn had visited. He whined, and Peter shot him another glare.

They seemed to be silent after that, so Gerard could only assume they used mind-speak. Excluded from the conversation, though, didn't mean he wasn't thinking himself, and the more he thought about it, the more he believed Bella was their main focus.

Without warning, her father stood. Aerowyn saw him out, then remained at the door, her shoulders sagging.

Gerard nudged her hand.

What were you discussing? I thought I heard Bella's name mentioned.

"Nothing you need to know about," Aerowyn said distractedly.

You seem a little worried.

"I am."

About what?

"To explain, I would have to tell you what my father and I were discussing." She went into the kitchen.

Gerard followed her.

Would that be so horrible for me to know?

"Yes and no. It involves your story also." She sat down at the table. "I don't think anyone should know too much about their future. Altering it could ruin it in the end."

Gerard sat on his haunches to watch her eyes, which shifted between blue and brown. Were sympathy and strategy waging a way in her heart?

How do Bella and that... He caught himself... *pirate relate to me?*

"It's complicated."

Gerard snorted. *I'm tired of all the mysteries. I want a chance to redeem my own path, now. If Bella and Jasper have something to do with it, let me in on the plan.*

Aerowyn looked away. She was hiding something. For a moment, he saw regret swirling in mind. She wanted him to be a man? And it was her fault that he wasn't?

Her eyes, now a rich chocolate-brown finally met his, and his stomach flipped. Her sky-blue eyes—Elayne's eyes—were his favorite, but they weren't truly blue. The color was a window to her true feelings.

"I want to give you the opportunity to redeem yourself, Gerard but now is not that time."

Something about her tone prompted him to ask a question he had never dared before.

Do you love me?

A myriad of emotions flashed across her face, and she stood abruptly to carry the tea pot to the stove. "That's not important right now."

Why isn't love important?

"Because this isn't about me. It's about saving many lives. If I selfishly try for my happy ending, many will lose out on theirs." She filled a floral-patterned bowl with water and set it in front of him. "I can't be responsible for that."

Her reply unsettled him. Had she unnecessarily tampered with many lives? He scrambled to his feet and paced the floor. *How are you to blame for anyone ending up miserable? How many have you cursed besides my brother and Jasper? You said they were selfish and deserved their enchantments.*

"I'm not directly to blame for all curses." She sat at the table and sipped her tea. "But I love my father too much to allow his choices to ruin more people's destinies. Helping him wrong his rights is my duty, and—my love for him binds me to this path."

You said you were teaching humans to be humble and kind. Are there any other fae doing this? I was under the impression it was the life mission of all fae.

"It's complicated. Let's just say the other fae didn't want to serve his objective, and now only Father and I are left to fix the mess that…"

She trailed off.

Gerard tilted his head to study her. Perhaps finishing the sentence felt like a betrayal, but Gerard saw it for what it was: a daughter's loyalty to and love for her father. Whatever Peter had done, she had made it her undertaking to fix the wrongs Peter set in motion. Her devotion was admirable, but it was unfair of her father to lure her in to solving his problems in the first place.

Gerard's own family would not have been less self-centered if Peter and Aerowyn hadn't interfered. Maybe there would have been fewer consequences. Who could possibly know that?

He was currently a wolf, but he wouldn't have been any happier as a man before Aerowyn manipulated his former life. Even if loving

Elayne had made him more complete despite losing her, yes, having only a moment of the love for Elayne was better than never experiencing true love at all.

Aerowyn brought the dishes to the sink and washed them by hand rather than magic. Gerard suspected she was avoiding his scrutiny. He sagging posture still gave away her gloomy mood even if he couldn't see her eyes.

He couldn't have admitted the importance of love right after she apparently died, but he had become wiser as a wolf. Or perhaps something else gave him this insight. Sometimes Aerowyn was the woman he loved, and other times she was a complete stranger, but as he spent time with her, he gained a deeper understanding.

But wherever that new knowledge came from Gerard wanted his old body back. As a man, he could help Aerowyn more than he was able to now.

He shoved philosophical musings aside so she wouldn't read them and lapped up some water from the bowl Aerowyn had put in front of him.

Since I can't know what you and your father discussed, what am I still doing here?

"For now, you're my companion. We'll be joining Jasper and Bella soon."

He whimpered. He'd forgotten about that girl in his own worries. *They're still sailing on that ship? Is she all right?*

"Yes, she's fine. Don't worry. She won't be with the pirate for much longer. Remember that matter I dealt with in New Orleans?"

Yes.

"That will soon re-direct Bella's path."

What the blazes? How many paths does Bella need to go on before you're done using her?

She startled. "Using... Why do you think I'm using her?"

Based on some of what I overheard you discuss with Peter and the fact that Bella has been involved in one way or another with two of the people you've cursed.

"Using is a strong word, because her life will change for the better too."

Gerard's tail twitched. If Bella's life improved, there was hope he could have a happy ending like Aerowyn had promised.

He blocked his thoughts from her.

If Aerowyn isn't a part of my story, I can't imagine it being perfectly happy.

Chapter 39

Jasper

The constant fear of running into the sea witch had distracted Jasper from the fact that they had been going in one large circle all night and day. He should have realized that since it took magic to enter the realm of Ageless Isle, the same element was needed to exit it. Despite Peter's claims that the golden sand would fly them back to his own world and despite Jasper's doubts, it was their only chance.

He glanced at the jar. "It's time to test the pixie dust."

"I can climb the mas' Cap'n," Jeb offered, "an' sprinkle that sparkly stuff onto the sails."

After a moment's thought, Jasper tossed the container to the tailor. Before Jeb began his ascent, however, another ship came into view. Soaring into the sky in front of another vessel wasn't a good idea. He didn't want to share any of his knowledge of magic. Besides, if the ship had valuable cargo, he'd plunder it and gain back the wealth lost to the hurricane.

"Wait, Jeb."

Jasper pulled out his spy-glass. An unfamiliar flag flew in the mast. It didn't belong to any country's navy, but it also didn't belong to any pirates Jasper knew, either. A silver sword shone against its emerald-green background. Either jealousy or chagrin had Jasper grinding his teeth. He hadn't remembered to think up a flag. Or perhaps Peter hadn't wanted to give them an ensign. True, he'd ordered Jeb to sew one, but a pennant hadn't been his priority. Escaping this bewitched sea had been. Now, however, Jasper wished Jeb had finished it. Surely everyone knew of his reputation. No ship should approach so brazenly.

"Wha, Cap'n?"

"Don't climb the mast yet. There's another ship approaching, and we want to keep our magical dust to ourselves." Jasper glanced around. Bella was nowhere to be seen, but he wasn't going to admit his plans out loud, just in case. "Perhaps they'll have some treasure we might barter for."

Jeb saluted. "Aye aye, Cap'n."

Although... if the ship was in this realm, they may already have some kind of magic. Bah. Jasper refused to worry about that. He raised his spyglass again. The other ship appeared to be a brigantine. His jaw tightened. The approaching vessel had more men.

His pirates, however, weren't afraid of a fight, and the crew knew what Jasper wanted. They grabbed their weapons and prepared for a potential battle. Jasper would talk his way around a dangerous situation. Charm and easy deception had gained him many fine acquisitions without blood-shed. His crew trusted him. He would never put them in a no-win position.

The ship glided toward them. Their captain shouted indiscernible orders, and they were loading their canons.

Sword in hand, Jasper signaled to Jeb. He barred his teeth and grunted. Intense and concentrated expression replaced relaxed ones. The pirates readied themselves for the clash.

When the brigantine floated near enough to board the *Black Fear II*, the captain—a young man close to Jasper's age—yelled, "Send Bella Bonnay over to our ship, and we will not fire upon you."

The hairs on Jasper's neck rose. This had to be another one of Peter or Aerowyn's tricks. No wonder Peter hadn't worried about Bella's safety. He had already planned her rescue.

Well, Jasper wasn't going to be manipulated into anything. They couldn't have her. He had promised to take her back unsullied, and that was what he was going to do.

He'd stand his ground and fight to the death.

Chapter 40

Bellarose

When Bella heard Jasper call out about an advancing ship, a tremor moved through her limbs—this was the next step in another dangerous adventure. Nevertheless, she climbed to the main deck to see for herself.

"Send Bella Bonnay over to our ship," the other captain shouted, "and we will not fire upon you."

She froze, one hand on the aft railing.

The man saw her. The ship was close enough that she saw lips curl into a smile that quickly faded. "Bella, is that you?"

An eerie feeling of déjà vu made the hairs on her arms stand on end, and his bold informality made her step backward. Strangers addressed her as Miss Bonnay, but... there was something familiar about the way he spoke her name.

Ever since Jasper had forced her to write the letters explaining that she had joined the *Black Fear's* crew by choice, she had doubted anyone would rescue her. At the beginning of the voyage, she had longed to be saved, but time had squelched that longing. Hope soared again. Maybe Brooke and Antoine had seen through the lies. Maybe Quinn would have too.

Or, maybe this was another one of Peter and Aerowyn's meddling ways.

Jasper approached and said quietly, though no one was around to hear, "Do you know who that is?"

She squinted to see the other captain better, but he was entirely unfamiliar. "I've never seen him before in my life. No one who knows where I am besides the de la Roses and Quinn. Besides, I was under the impression no one from our world would be able to reach us without magic."

Jasper avoided eye contact with Bella as he exhaled. "I have been thinking the same thing. Since we're near Ageless Island, I suspect Aerowyn or Peter have something to do with this."

"Yes, me too. I'm uncertain what either of the fae have planned, but I don't trust this."

"Unless maybe another scoundrel has heard of your beauty and wants to take you from me." Jasper rubbed his hook as he looked back at the captain. "Perhaps he thinks he can get something for you. You know, pirates don't just barter with treasure. I find selling humans more work than its worth, but that young captain may gain a great sum for selling you to the highest bidder."

Bile rose to Bella's throat. "I hope you're teasing me, but even if you aren't, that captain can't be from our world. The ship was brought here by magic, and for that to be true, Aerowyn or Peter must be involved."

"You're right. That settles it." Jasper spun away from her to call out to the other captain, "Who are you to make such demands? Bella is better off with me than on your ship."

The captain pulled out a sword. "I have it on good authority that Miss Bonnay didn't join your crew voluntarily. She was kidnapped and will want to join me. I will return her safely to her friends in New Orleans."

Bella trembled at the words.

That confirms our suspicions.

Besides Jasper, Sven was the only one who knew the details of Bella's reason for being on the *Black Fear*. She wanted to believe that this outsider was trustworthy, but she didn't. She couldn't.

Jasper had promised Peter to take her to New Orleans. He said he was no longer interested in making her his mistress, and she believed him. His test in Treasure Lagoon had changed him. She saw the way he had looked at Cerise and it was unmistakable who had his full attention. Maybe even his heart.

She was safe enough where she was.

The stranger raised his voice. "May I come over to discuss this without shouting?"

Jasper eyed Bella, and she nodded.

"Leave your weapons behind," Jasper yelled.

The brigantine's captain sheathed his sword and took off his belt. His men connected his ship to the *Black Fear II* with long planks. He jumped up onto it effortlessly and walked over the ocean to stand in front of Bella. The warm sunlight on his brown hair revealed copper highlights. She tilted her head to look up at him since he was as tall as Jasper. She blinked twice because his warm brown eyes reminded her of Quinn's.

Bella swallowed back her apprehension. "How do you know anything about me, and how do I know I can trust you?"

The man squared his shoulders. "My lady, it isn't necessary for you to know how I received this information. What you must accept is that I am your only chance to return home unmarred."

Unmarred? Good heavens. Bella didn't like his choice of words.

"I don't have a home. I wrote a letter to the people I left behind in Louisiana stating that I wanted to be here. They think I'm on this ship by choice." She folded her shaking hands behind her back. "I suspect an enchantress sent you here, and I don't know if I can trust her either."

The other captain's expression soured. "Are you saying you rather sail with this pirate who kidnapped you than come back to New Orleans with me?"

Bella's eyes darted between the two men. "Jasper agreed to take me back there safely."

"And you trust him?"

Jasper shoved between them. "You might say Bella and I have come to an understanding."

Bella clenched her jaw. It was one thing to semi-trust Jasper, but it was entirely another to give this stranger the impression she had succumbed to the pirate's charms. She didn't want anyone to think she was his mistress.

"Besides," Jasper continued before she thought of a way to contradict erroneous assumptions, "you threatened to fire your canons on the *Black Fear II* if I don't surrender Bella. Does that mean you are prepared to see her go down with my ship? Wouldn't that ruin your rescue?"

The strange captain stiffened, "I wouldn't have allowed Miss Bonnay to sink with your ship." His head turned to his men and then back at Jasper. "I am prepared to end this parley with you if you don't agree to allow Miss Bonnay to come with me now."

"No one threatens me and gets away with it." Jasper shoved Bella back behind him. "We will duel for who is allowed to give Bella passage to New Orleans."

The brigantine's captain yelled, "Board and seize!"

Jasper's sword swung from its sheath on his baldric, and another flew through the air. The other captain caught and raised his it in time to block Jasper's swing.

Men from the mystery ship fired guns, and other sailors scrambled aboard the *Black Fear II*. The pirate's crew fired their pistols at the invaders. Metal clanged, and the smell of gun powder filled the air.

Fear crawled up Bella's spine and threatened to engulf her. Jasper's men were outnumbered and couldn't win. She edged away from the men, but she couldn't stop staring at the captains' flashing blades.

Thrust, cut, lunge, and repeat.

Clang, retreat, parry, and feint—repeat.

Bella stared transfixed. Oddly, something about the stranger's footwork and movements reminded her of Quinn.

Jasper's men were outnumbered three to two, and the longer they fought the more evident they were not the victors.

At last, breathless, sweat-soaked, and bloodied from a gash in his arm, Jasper threw down his sword and yelled, "Cease, men! We surrender!"

Metal clattered on wood as the defeated crew dropped their weapons.

While the brigantine's captain and crew took away the pirates' blades, Bella fought back worry. Why had Jasper risked the battle? Yes, he'd always given her the impression he would rather die than bow down to his enemy, but the *Black Fear II's* limited crew had no chance against the larger ship.

True, Jasper was a dishonorable villain, but he was smart enough to know his reputation wasn't enough to conquer his enemy.

Once the *Black Fear II's* men were under control, the brigantine's captain turned to his ship, and Bella's stomach knotted. Aerowyn herself slid across the other ship's deck with a large black wolf by her side. *Gerard!* Bella fisted her hands. Poor Gerard was still stuck as an animal and Aerowyn's companion.

Anger mixed with fear surged inside Bella. No one was completely safe with the unpredictable enchantress orchestrating lives and if it wasn't obvious before, it certainly was now.

Even if Jasper had a thousand pirates fighting, he wouldn't have conquered the brigantine's crew. Aerowyn's presence confirmed all Bella's suspicions, and a lump formed in her throat.

Aerowyn crossed the planks to the *Black Fear II*.

Her violet eyes narrowed at Jasper.

"Captain Falcon, we meet again."

Bella blinked in confusion. Didn't Aerowyn have brown eyes? Hadn't they seemed warm and kind, even when she had just turned Gerard into a wolf?

"Ah." Jasper's mouth pinched, then he gave a heartless smile. "The crafty enchantress—or should I call you Princess Aerowyn? You are King Peter's daughter, aren't you?"

"Yes," she said, "but you need not address me with my titles. Father is more particular about those things than I am."

"Didn't you already have your fun with me when that dog chomped off my hand?" Jasper lifted his hook. A few of the other crew drew back and Jasper growled out, "Why do you need to steal my ship?"

Aerowyn's cold gaze fastened on Jasper with such intensity that Bella backed up a step. "I warned you that your actions will have consequences, and Captain Modo is here to enforce payment for your misdeeds. If you want to be technical, it really isn't your ship, but we don't want the *Black Fear II*. We're here for Bella."

Jasper huffed. "With all that powerful magic at your disposal, why would you need this Captain Modo's help? Is he fae too?"

"My reasons are none of your con—"

A whirlpool opened up, and the deck tilted. Water rushed. sweeping the two ships toward a dark mouth. Aerowyn stumbled and rolled into the ocean. Gerard howled and dove after Aerowyn.

Crew members of both ships managed to keep their balance, and a distant part of Bella's brain struggled to understand how Aerowyn, an enchantress, could be so easily swept away. The ship lurched again, and Bella grabbed Jasper's arm to stay upright.

Waves crashed over the deck, soaking Bella with salt water and chilling to her bones. What had been a warm tropical ocean only moments before turned into a stormy winter sea. Bella shook from terror and being drenched in frigid water. Her horror amplified when a slick chartreuse eel with a woman's upper body rose from the churning vortex. The eel-woman's tubular body was as large as two men tied together and a tuft of seaweed-like hair sprouted from her head.

"Callista!" Jasper screamed. "The sea witch!"

With a jarring crash, the ships rammed into one another. Another wave hit, sweeping men into the ocean. Bella lost her grip on Jasper, but he grabbed her with his good hand and pulled her to the riggings. She held on to the ropes with frozen fingers, and he braced himself against the storm, his hook around the thick ropes.

If Aerowyn hadn't been washed away, she could have stopped the storm.

Within seconds, Bella's fingers lost grip of the slippery ropes.

Jasper shouted her name.

Boards and sails flew past. Her palms burned as a wave tossed her across the rigging. She slammed into wood and ropes, and then her bruised and bloodied body was slung into the churning water.

She kicked to get her head above the foaming waves and gasped for breath when she surfaced. A strong sinewy arm wrapped around her, and someone pulled her through the chilly water and up to safety. Who?

She dashed the seawater out of her eyes.

Somehow Captain Modo swam through the storm and dragged her back to his ship. If he wasn't one of the fae, Aerowyn had gifted him with supernatural abilities because no other explanation fit the miraculous rescue.

Another jolt, and the ships separated. The vessels stopped rocking, but the storm raged between them. The rest of the sea had gone dead calm.

Gerard's black head bobbed up, then sank beneath the water. His barks were weak as he fought to stay afloat.

Bella rasped out, "Gerard!" She coughed and made eye-contact with the captain. "Please save him."

Captain Modo jumped into the ocean again and pulled the wolf to the brigantine. His crew quickly created a makeshift hammock and lifted the wolf onto the main deck. Gerard growled but didn't harm his rescuers. He pounced onto the deck and turned immediately to face the side.

Bella pivoted and gasped.

There, in the eye of the whirlpool, Aerowyn was wrestling with Callista. Only the color of skin, electricity, and clothing could be seen in the fight. Light-blue fought yellow-green as Aerowyn's arms yanked on Callista's. The witch reached a long, chartreuse arm and snatched pendant from the enchantress's neck.

A flash of the necklace on another girl's neck arced through Bella's memory.

I found a book of spells, and then this appeared around my neck. I think it gives me magical abilities when I'm inside here.

A shout shattered the recollection and drew her attention to the other ship. Jeb was pointing to the churning ocean—where Jasper fought his way through the water, a knife between his teeth. His bulging muscles cut through the waves.

Bella watched him with growing horror.

Gerard growled and paced, but he stayed aboard.

Was Jasper going to kill one or both of the witches? Would he rather end their lives than stay safely aboard his ship? Did he think that if he destroyed the sorceresses, he could save his ship?

When Aerowyn's sister died, her magic died with her, but Jasper hadn't read that story.

She wrapped her arms around her middle.

You are in the middle of a crisis, Bellarose! Why must you always refer to a story?

Maybe... Maybe because I am... inside a book?

No, she must have knocked her head before falling into the ocean. Being inside a tale was as ridiculous as Jasper risking his life to kill an immortal.

Chapter 41

Jasper

Jasper's throat and eyes burned as he pushed through the salt water. His vision blurred, but he saw Captain Modo save Bella. She hadn't drowned.

He slowed and tread the water for a moment, his focus on the duo in the center of the whirlpool. The sea monster scratched Aerowyn's face with her clawed fingernails, and Aerowyn wailed but pushed the witch's hands away from her face.

They fought without magic.

Think, Jasper. Think.

If he tried to get back on his ship, the storm would continue, but killing Callista, might end her magic or at least give Aerowyn a chance to calm the ocean.

Jasper had the advantage of surprise. He could reach them before they noticed while they fought. He pulled his knife from its sheath under his pant leg and tucked it between his teeth to free his arms for swimming. Could plain, cold steel pierce an eel-woman's body?

There wasn't time to worry about that.

He swam with all his might. Every part of his body ached, and he missed his hand more than ever. The hook couldn't pull him through the waves the same way. Stroke after stroke, he forced his way through water and the pain. The waves seemed to aid him toward his goal.

"Your father ruined my life," Callista screeched over the thundering whitecaps. "Now I'm going to devastate his by killing you!" She yanked on the chain from Aerowyn's neck and flung it into the ocean.

A prolonged wolf's howl sounded from the distance.

"Callista, why are you doing this?" Aerowyn coughed and spat a mouthful of seawater. "I don't want to hurt you. I don't have any quarrel with you."

"You think you've won?" Callista gloated. "Your necklace is gone! You have no powers!"

"You're wrong." Aerowyn held up her arms, and the raging sea calmed in seconds.

Callista screamed in frustration.

A chill deeper than the cold of the storm swept over Jasper. His plan to kill Callista wasn't going to work if these two could work magic after all.

"How?" Callista wailed and beat the water with her fists. "I took away your pendant!"

"Jasper!"

Callista stopped suddenly, her eyes fixed on Jasper. And then something else behind him.

He turned.

Cerise!

She made her way through the waves toward him, concern on her beautiful face.

"No, Cerise! Dive!"

She didn't listen. He swam toward her as fast as he could, but before he could reach her, magic stole Jasper's knife out of his teeth and flung it into Cerise's heart.

The blade made contact. Cerise's beautiful green eyes went wide. And out of the corner of his eye, Jasper saw the witch disappear below the surface.

With every bit of strength he had, Jasper carved his way through the whitecaps to her side as the mermaid's blood reddened the now glassy water.

The dagger that punctured her heart disintegrated into sea foam. He had only his hand to plug the cavity it left behind. Jasper struggled futilely to stop the bleeding but she went limp.

"Aerowyn," he cried. "Heal her!"

Aerowyn reached them. "If she were human, I could, but she is a magical creature, and this wound has been caused by something other than your knife."

Confused and frantic, Jasper pulled Cerise into his hooked arm—careful not to injure her with the sharp appendage. He kept the wound covered with his only hand and pumped his legs to stay afloat. He applied as much pressure as he could while he bobbed up and down in the sea.

"Cerise," Jasper begged, but she didn't respond. He looked at Aerowyn. "Why is the hole so huge?"

Without a word, Aerowyn waved a scepter, though he hadn't seen it before. Jasper and Cerise floated onto the deck of the brigantine where Bella and Captain Modo stood with open mouths. Gerard ran up to Aerowyn and nudged her.

"You have to save her!" Jasper pleaded, his normal self-control ripped away. His long-buried emotions for Cerise rose to crush him, and tears coursed down his cheeks.

"Where is that witch? Get her! Make her reverse the curse!"

"I can't save her, and neither can Callista. Only the heart of her true love can." Aerowyn knelt down to face him. "It needs to happen before it's too late. If the ceremonial magic isn't performed soon, she will die and turn into sea foam."

"If you can save her, do it now!" Jasper barked out.

Gerard emitted a low growl.

Aerowyn's cool blue eyes turned brown. "It can only be done with her true love."

"Who is that?"

Aerowyn placed her hand on Jasper's tattooed forearm while his hand remained firmly over Cerise's wound. "You know who that is."

Him? Of course he loved her, but could she love him? Even if it was an impossible, small chance, Jasper's throat tightened in panic, and he swallowed hard. "Yes, I love her, but what can I do? How can I help?"

"You will have to give up your humanity and share half of your heart with her. Understand, you will become an immortal merman. The price for this magic is that you both will be creatures of the sea forever—unable to return to land—no legs, only fins."

Jasper already wanted that, but what if she didn't want to be forever stuck under the sea? What if she didn't love him—rejected his love?

"Jasper," Aerowyn said sternly, "we're running out of time. I know you're afraid she doesn't want half of your heart, but that is the risk you take when you love someone. This is your only opportunity to redeem yourself and get your hand back."

The hooked appendage was the last thing on his mind. He didn't even care about redemption for all his past horrific deeds. All he cared about was that the one who already captured his heart lived.

"Do it now! Take my whole heart and give it to her. She can have the whole thing if it means the world still has her in it." His voice cracked from emotion. "You must save her, please."

"I only need half your heart for the spell. You will be forced to become a merman. It is part of the payment to break the curse. All magic comes with a price."

"Do it," he said without hesitation. "Now."

Aerowyn spoke in a language like the one Peter used to call Tilly, and a bluish glow encircled her hands. A strange, melodic siren song vibrated through the air. Then, she reached inside Jasper's chest and pulled out his heart.

He only felt pressure rather than pain from the intrusion. There was no blood, but only a hole in his chest. The red organ pumped in the palm of her hand and continued to thrum while she molded it into a different shape, like a potter with clay.

Jasper sat quietly in awe, somehow breathing without his heart. He focused on Cerise. A buzz of energy he couldn't identify seeped through him, and he felt a peace beyond understanding.

Aerowyn then split Jasper's heart in half, and the pieces rose from her hands to float in mid-air, bathed in the blue light. With freed hands, the enchantress pulled out Cerise's heart. Black veins spread from the gaping wound where the dagger had pierced it.

Aerowyn whispered, "The black is poison running through her heart. That is the curse Callista used to kill Cerise if no sacrifice was made."

The enchantress grabbed Jasper's heart halves and simultaneously put one part in Cerise's chest and the other half in his. They gasped loudly at the same time. The siren song pierced Jasper. It surrounded the sections and pumped blue light through both their bodies.

The hole in his chest and hers closed. A new tingling sensation climbed up his toes, up into his legs. A painless vibration deep in his bones tore his skin.

Jasper's breeches ripped and a blackish iridescent fin replaced his legs. His hook vanished, and his hand returned.

Cerise lovely eyes fluttered open. She met his eyes, and he couldn't help but smile.

Suddenly Jasper's lungs closed, and he couldn't breathe. Sharp, unimaginable pain grabbed his chest, and instinct told him he needed to get into the ocean. Cerise must have felt the same way, for color drained from her face. She thrashed her red tail while gulping for air she couldn't take in.

Jasper pulled Cerise to him, held her with one arm and flipped both of them over the railing of Captain Modo's ship.

They splashed into the ocean. Immediately, water soothed away the searing pain. Water and bubbles whooshed, and Aerowyn swam toward them, her legs transformed into a mermaid fin. Cerise's eyes widened. Fear and something Jasper couldn't decipher was written on her face.

Aerowyn held out a hand, and Cerise shrank against Jasper's side.

"What happened? I was swimming to help you, Jasper, when, when... I can't remember."

"Callista hexed Jasper's dagger, and drove it through your heart. The only choices you had were death or to receive half the heart of true love." Aerowyn gestured to Jasper. "He gave you part of his heart, but as you know, magic has a price."

"No!" Cerise cried out, and Jasper's stomach sank. "What was the price?"

"Neither of you can return to land ever again. You will forever live under the sea."

Sunlight reached Cerise's hair, which shone like fire. Her earnest green eyes darted between Aerowyn and him.

Her unreadable expression worried Jasper. Would she have rather died than be stuck in the ocean permanently?

"My job here is done. I'm glad you chose correctly." Aerowyn disappeared, without a single bubble left behind.

Jasper breathed in cool water. He didn't regret his decision. Perhaps one day the crimes he'd committed would be washed away. Perhaps one day she would accept his love.

He braced himself for her rejection.

Chapter 42

Gerard

Gerard was relieved to see Aerowyn return safely to Captain Modo's ship. She whisked them back to Ageless Isle before there was time to ask any questions.

She must've known how Gerard was feeling because she sighed before she asked, "Why are you so agitated?"

Besides the fact that I'm still a wolf? You almost died. I was helpless to aide you in that storm! I hate being so useless.

She smiled, which didn't help his temper. "It only looked as if I almost died, but the only way I can be killed is by dragon fire. You know that."

I also thought the only way you remained immortal and kept your magic was when you wore that pendant. When Callista took it, I was terrified. I assumed you would lose your powers and be able to die. Why did you still have your magic? Is it in that wand you use?

She folded her hands and put both index fingers to her lips. "The wand only helps me aim my magic more accurately toward its target. But my father has been keeping secrets from me. He finally told me why Callista was so angry, but even then, he didn't tell me the pendant was useless. I guess there is more for me to discover."

Gerard paced the room, trying to absorb the effects of father's deeds and lies. Too exhausted by the day's events, he rotated and settled with a grunt on his mattress. Aerowyn sat on the floor next to him and brushed his fur clean of salt water and grime. He slowly relaxed.

"I haven't been to the Kingdom of Magic since Father and I left. They wouldn't want to see me after what Father had done to them." She stopped brushing and leaned back against the wall. "The fae didn't want to be ruled by my father's tyranny and left Ageless Isle."

But they all have magic and are immortal?

"Perhaps they do. I still have my magic, after all, but immortality takes years to prove."

Immortality isn't as important as justice, so tell, me, Aerowyn. Why did that pirate get his happy ending before me when I sacrificed for my only brother? I would do it again, but that man is a wretched pirate, yet he winds up with his true love?

"These things take time." She shook her head. "Jasper's redemption came sooner than I had planned because of Callista's interference."

He eyed her.

What was the original plan?

"I suppose I can tell you now that it is all over." Aerowyn grabbed a cushion from a nearby chair and scooted onto it. "Captain Modo and Jasper were to fight. Modo would have won with my help, and Jasper would have been on the brink of death."

Gerard huffed.

"I knew Cerise and Jasper belonged under the sea together where he could no longer hurt anyone. She only needed the opportunity to save him. It was going to be half of Cerise's heart that I planned to use to save Jasper's life. He would have still been forced to become a permanent merman."

You thought she would give half her heart to save that scum?

Gerard growled quietly.

"She already had given her whole heart with her love. Years ago, when she was a mergirl and he a little boy, she met Jasper when he ran away from home. He never forgot her kindness though he thought it was a dream."

As a boy, I'm sure he was fine, but he turned out to be vicious.

Aerowyn met his eyes. "Don't forget how pain molded you."

Gerard snorted.

"Cerise knew there was hope for Jasper, and she made it her mission to help him find a better life. She followed his ship around the world."

That means she witnessed him murder and plunder, and yet she still loved him?

"Yes." Aerowyn rested her hand on his back. "Mermaids read feelings and motives. She knew what he had buried deeper than any treasure chest—what he hid even from himself."

I still think his near-death would have been better than hers. I know what she did for Bella that first time, saving her from Callista's storm.

"His story had been altered because of my father's actions. His parents weren't supposed to be abusive, but loving." She rubbed her temples. "Jasper should have gone into an honorable career and become an admiral for the Continental Navy instead of joining a pirate crew. My father created Callista and the dragons that killed his parents' parents."

Gerard bolted to his feet. *Your father created a dragon? Like the one that killed your sister? That's beyond anything Jasper or I have done.*

Sadness filled her eyes. "Yes. I've only recently learned part of what my father has done to alter the tales, but that small part makes me determined to help him fix the stories before more lives are ruined."

What is my part in all of this? I was useless today as a wolf.

"The time is coming when I will need your help. Have patience, Gerard. Your tale isn't over yet."

He had been patient. Now Gerard wanted results.

Chapter 43

Bellarose

B ella's breath hitched. Jasper and Cerise disappeared into the ocean, and Aerowyn followed them. When she returned, she touched Gerard, and they both vanished into thin-air.

Bella turned to Captain Modo, who was staring at her. "Now what?"

He looked away, over the waves. "We return to New Orleans."

"But that's in a different world. You'll need magic to get there. I assume it was Aerowyn who brought you here in the first place?"

He nodded. "Yes, but she gifted me with what I need to return you safely."

"What about Jasper's men? They are without a captain."

The pirates paced the *Black Fear II's* decks. Without Jasper's leadership, they would be like fish out of water. None of them were adequate to take the captain's role.

"They can become a part of the *Notre Dame*," Captain Modo offered.

Then, he yelled over to the *Black Fear II*, "If you wish, you may join my crew. You will have to follow my rules, and we won't kill or plunder to gain wealth." He stood stiffly. "You will earn a decent wage and you will have a bed and food aboard my ship."

The pirates talked amongst themselves.

Jeb responded for all of them. "Aye, Cap'n Modo, we'd like to come wif you back to Orleans where the mens and me 'ope to find a diff'ren' ship more suited to us."

Captain Modo grimaced, but relayed his answer with dignity. "That will suffice. You may leave my crew after we drop Miss Bonnay off, but remember that any acts of piracy are punishable by death upon this ship. I will not allow it."

"Yes, Cap'n."

The pirates saluted, then lined up to swing on the riggings onto the *Notre Dame*. Captain Modo's men led the pirates below where Bella assumed they would get proper uniforms and be able to peel off their worn, odorous clothes.

The *Notre Dame's* sails billowed, and as she left, the vacant *Black Fear II* behind the pirate ship evaporated before Bella's eyes.

"Did you see that?" she asked the captain.

"Yes." His eyes widened. "I guess the spell used to create it was no longer necessary."

"It seems suspicious," she said. "Now that we no longer need it, the ship conveniently disappears." She debated what to share with this stranger, but then added. "Jasper and I believed Peter, Aerowyn's father, created the vessel. He said we crafted it with our imaginations, but I don't think we did."

Captain Modo faced her. "You don't trust the fae?"

"Not really." She bit her lip and turned away. His brown eyes were distracting since they reminded her of Quinn, which now that she thought of it, his surname, Modo, was the same as Quinn's. What were the odds?

After several minutes, then he said, "Aerowyn led me to believe you were kidnapped and Captain Falcon wanted you to become a permanent member of his crew. Why was he going to return you to New Orleans?"

"Ageless Isle changed Jasper." She shifted her weight to give him a half smile. "The place wasn't what any of us expected."

"What do you mean?"

"Jasper sought riches galore, but instead, he found terror."

The captain crossed his hands behind him but leaned into her words. "What kind of terrors?"

"I don't know, exactly, because they happened to him when he was alone, but he couldn't get off the island fast enough. There were some dangerous mythical creatures, and all the pirates had to pass tests." She turned and saw a bench. She sat down, and Captain Modo sat beside her.

"I don't know what Aerowyn told you about Jasper, but he had less... than honorable intentions when he kidnapped me. After Ageless Isle, he stopped trying to seduce me." She breathed in the briny air. "Perhaps he had already fallen in love with Cerise. She helped us in the first storm Callista threw at us, but I didn't think he could fall in love that fast."

Captain Modo eyed her oddly, then returned his gaze to the ocean.

Bella watched him out of the corner of her eye. What had prompted her to tell the man that? What must he think of her now? He was stern, nonsensical, and somehow empathetic. It was hard to understand what it was about the man that put her at ease enough to share so much information. The man was a stranger, yet familiar.

"Are you assessing me?" Captain Modo asked.

Since he was facing the sea, how did he see her looking him over?

"Yes, I suppose. After being kidnapped, I haven't felt entirely safe. Since Aerowyn enlisted your help for this mission, I don't know if I can trust you, either, but here I am over-sharing what happened on my journey."

He turned and gave her a half smile. "I don't mind hearing about it."

"There is some reason that the enchantress and her father wanted me to be a part of these adventures while they punished the people they deemed selfish or vain."

Captain Modo's lips became a straight line. "Were you actually kidnapped? The letters your friends received told a different narrative."

"You just told me Aerowyn had explained that fact to you." Bella fidgeted with her fingers.

"And you just told me you don't trust her. Neither do I."

"That is fair. Yes, Jasper forced me to write those letters." Bella's temples throbbed at the memory. "He said he would kill my— my— he said he would kill Quinn if I didn't write them."

A strange expression washed over the captain's face.

He shifted. "Who's Quinn?"

There was no way on land or water that Bella would share what Quinn really meant to her, not even to this kind but confusing captain. "He was a man who protected me when I first arrived in New Orleans and Jasper found a way to use that against me. Quinn has the same surname as you. Do you have any relatives in New Orleans?"

"You keep calling the pirate Jasper, as if you two became friendly." His scowl made Bella feel uncomfortable and made her forget her last question. "If he hadn't fallen in love with a mermaid, perhaps you would have stayed on his ship?"

She glared at him. "What are you insinuating?"

"It's what he implied. Captain Falcon said you had come to an *understanding*."

"He lied!" Her face was on fire, and she clenched her fists. "I never gave in to any of his advances—ever!"

"I didn't mean to offend you, Miss Bonnay," the captain said quickly. "I'm sorry. You seemed unwilling to leave him when I told you I came to rescue you."

"It was because I didn't know who was more dangerous, you or Jasper. I had never met you before and at least Jasper was acting civilly." She huffed. "Anyway, since I'm no longer a rich girl, I'd rather not use titles. Please call me Bella."

The captain blushed. She expected him to tell her his first name, but he remained silent. Rude.

But then, Gerard, the man she thought was abominably selfish, sacrificed himself for his brother. Quinn had seemed to love her, but he hadn't joined Jasper's crew. And Jasper. What an unexpected twist. A vile pirate turned into a hero. His transformation into a merman was miraculous, but that was commonplace compared to his sacrifice for Cerise.

All the twisted turns she had experienced after leaving France had taught her that people could change. Her narrow-minded first impressions and assumptions were hardly ever accurate.

Perhaps she shouldn't judge this captain harshly, either.

Captain Modo broke the silence. "I'd rather continue to call you Miss Bonnay. I do not wish to give the men the wrong idea of our relationship. I will not presume anything about your relationship with Captain Falcon', if you try not to presuppose anything about me."

She managed to smile. "That's not what I expected you to say, but I'm realizing that people are rarely what their first impressions show me."

"Indeed." Captain Modo stood. "This will be a long journey. It's possible we will get to know each other quite well. Until then, would you like me to show you to your room?"

There was that familiar feeling in Captain Modo's smile again, warming her to her toes.

She hadn't ever met this man, had she?

Bella stood too fast to follow him to her room. Stars entered her vision. She was going to faint, and she—

The world went blank.

To her chagrin, Bella was back inside that library from another time. She must have embarrassingly blacked out on a ship with the handsome Captain Modo as witness because this dream world appeared every time she lost consciousness, and there was Hobbes, the cat, sniffing her face.

She jumped to her feet and dashed to the library doors, but instead of finding the *Notre Dame*, she came upon another room of bookshelves. She ran through that to the next room. And the next. It was as if the library grew.

Bella's mouth went dry, but when she longed for fresh water, an ice-cold glass of water appeared in her hand. Thirst beat out the rising panic at the impossibilities. This wasn't Ageless Isle. Or was it?

Bella's mind whirled. "I need to sit down. Am I dreaming or did Peter move me off the ship? Or... I'm inside a story! None of this is real!"

What was real was her home with her parents in the shabby apartment building. If she could only get back to the original, ornate room where she left Layney, then maybe she could get out of this adventure and return to her real home, the Castle Creek Apartments.

Layney? She reminded her of someone else...

She dashed back the way she came and finally reached a room with a scene painted on a ceiling. White, billowing clouds swirled around black, star-studded skies with sparkly dust mingling with all of it. A phoenix blazed in and out of the scene beside a fire-breathing dragon. Each time one mythical creature vanished into the clouds another one appeared, creating the illusion that the white puffy nebulas were their normal habitat.

"What the fudge?" Bella said aloud.

A plate full of fudge appeared next to her. It was like the glass of water. Somehow the room had taken her literally and sent candy.

Layney. She was the girl who introduced her to this library that produced treats from thin air. Then she remembered the boys, Gerard and Quinn, who also lived at Castle Creek apartments.

But which was the book, and which was real?

"How do I get out of here?"

There was no answer.

If she had been trapped in a tale, what about the others? What if they were trapped as well?

What had she been reading? The memories came back and she demanded, "Take me to the fairy tales."

The contemporary room with its clean lines and colors disappeared, and she was in a new room. The air made her skin feel tingly as if she sensed the magic at work. If she hadn't been so freaked out by being ensnared eternally in a world that really didn't exist, she would have loved this room.

Joyful holiday music played quietly in the background. Bella wondered if Christmas would arrive while she was inside this library, but Layney said time didn't pass while she read. But if she came from a fairy tale and was trapped in a library, maybe she needed to go back into the fairy tale until it was completed.

She rubbed her temples. It was all so confusing.

Brooke and Antoine had their happily ever after, or at least Bella assumed they would. Gerard's story wasn't over because he couldn't remain a wolf forever, and he needed to escape back to the real world too. Then there was Quinn. She had really cared for him, even if she had never found out what happened to him.

Bella, the girl in the story, wanted Quinn to love her. Of course, he wasn't the Quinn Bella met at Castle Creek Apartments. He had commented on *A Christmas Carol,* one of her own favorite holiday tales. Her feelings were all jumbled.

On a hunch, Bella asked the library for a story about Captain Modo and the *Notre Dame.* Bella's eyes widened as it floated in the air to her. She sat in the cozy recliner and opened up the book. Hobbes, the orange tabby jumped up onto her lap, purred, and curled into a ball.

She turned the page and began to read.

"Miss Bonnay? Miss Bonnay, are you alright?"

Bella woke up to warm brown eyes of an unfamiliar face.

"What happened?"

"You fainted when you stood too suddenly, and when you fell, you hit your head hard. You're on the *Notre Dame.*"

Briny wind hit her face, and Bella sat up on the ship's hard planks.

"Yes... I remember. Aerowyn defeated Callista, and Jasper and Cerise are gone..." She also remembered the captain's strong arm around her as he rescued her from the ocean. Had she been dreaming? Remnants of the wonderful dream had disappeared.

Modo's brows knit together. "Miss Bonnay, why don't I take you to your room where you can freshen up and rest."

"That's probably best." She stood with the captain's assistance. "I don't know how long I was blacked out, but I had a dream."

"It wasn't that long," Captain Modo replied. "If you could follow me, Miss Bonnay, I think you'll like your room."

"What I would really like is for a short uneventful trip back to New Orleans," she said, and the captain almost cracked a smile.

Maybe someday she would remember the vision and write it down. She would return home to New Orleans, explain everything to her friends, and maybe have a second chance to talk to Quinn.

In her heart, Bella just knew the visions were perfect content for another magical story. But for now, she'd wish upon the stars that her journey would be uneventful, Captain Modo wouldn't be too much of a drag, and that Quinn would be happy to see her when she reached New Orleans.

Chapter 44

Jasper

The vivid colors of the ocean surrounding Jasper were nothing compared to the face from his dreams. She was real, and she was alive. He'd have a lifetime to explore the underwater world, but currently Jasper's concentration was on Cerise.

With a weakened voice that still reminded him of music, Cerise asked, "Jasper, do you love me?"

Inside his chest, his strange heart thumped faster. "I tried not to, but I couldn't help myself."

"But you don't really know me."

"You were kind to me even when I didn't deserve it. You saved me from myself. You filled a different kind of hole in my heart that I didn't realize I had."

Cerise raised one eyebrow. "When you were seven, you told me that you loved me, but I didn't know if you remembered that."

"I thought it was a dream until you showed up and saved Bella."

She reached for his hands. "I was born with a special gift to see inside a person's heart, and I saw past all the hate and cruelty. Your broken heart was capable of love. I wanted it, but I knew it was impossible. I tried to stay away, but I wanted to be part of your world."

Jasper squeezed her hands. "I wanted to be part of your world too." He pulled her closer.

Cerise's laugh was even more musical underwater. "Then we both got what we wanted."

She wrapped her arms around his waist, and he pulled her to him. Her tiny frame disappeared inside his large embrace. She gazed at him, and they floated in the ocean currents, mesmerized in each other's eyes.

Jasper bent and pressed his mouth to hers in a kiss like none he had ever experienced, and his half-heart beat rapidly in time with hers.

She whispered against his lips, "Jasper Falcon, I love you."

"And I love you back."

Cerise pulled back but kept his hand in hers. "Now it's time for you to see my home."

She flipped her fin in a flirtatious way, and he followed.

His cheeks hurt from smiling, but he didn't care.

Jasper called behind her, "Wait!"

She stopped, and he caught up to her.

"If you can really read my heart, you know that I already found my home in you." He pulled her into his arms again. "You're the home, security, and treasure I had always pirated for."

Love surged through his heart and Jasper knew the moment he had chosen to love Cerise, that he had found the X on the treasure map of his heart.

Letter & About Author

Dear Book Dragon,

Do you trust me? I promise this story will have an ending in the next book, "Bellarose and the Captain". Thank you for following this journey. Both Bella, Quinn, Aerowyn, and Gerard will have their finales and there will be happily ever afters. As Aerowyn said, "Have patience."

Go ahead rate, review and tell anyone you can about my stories. Every thing helps!

Always Imagining, Carla Reighard

ABOUT

Carla Reighard lives with her husband and three cats, Han, Leia, and Kylo, who all attempt to "help" when she's crafting a new saga. Fairies, mermaids, talking animals, and supernatural bicycles were her childhood companions, but until the publication of *Elle's Magical Shoes*, they remained inside her head. If you're bold enough to read fairy tales and brave enough to believe in redemption, you've found the right book. See more of her work at https://carlareighard.com.

instagram.com/carlareighard/

goodreads.com/author/show/7085189.Carla_Reighard

facebook.com/people/Carla-Reighard/61567154826280/